The Passion of Man

Happiness & Fulfillment Through God-Centered Relationship!

By

Darrell Johnson, Ph.D.

Cover design by Jay Cookingham

Email inquiries: www.ctsministries.com

Copyright © 2005, Darrell Johnson, Ph.D.

All rights reserved. No part of this publication may be reproduced, stored in a retrieval system, or transmitted in any form or by any means, electronic, mechanical, photocopying, recording, or otherwise, without the prior written permission of the publisher.

ISBN: 0-9769957-2-7

Published by:
Holy Fire Publishing
531 Constitution Blvd. Martinsburg, WV 25401
www.ChristianPublish.com

Printed in the United States of America and the United Kingdom

Acknowledgements

I dedicate this book to Jesus Christ, my Lord and Savior. I offer my deepest gratitude for inspiring, encouraging, and guiding me throughout the journey of penning the words contained in this book.

I also dedicate the fruits of my labor resulting in the publishing of this book to: my dearest Paulette (you are indeed the *"love of my life"*!), Marcus (you embody what a father would desire in a son), Jasmine (the Lord is only getting started with you Princess), Joy (the light of your spirit shines bright in the lives of everyone you touch), and Jade (your kind, humble, unassuming spirit is a true inspiration and joy).

Special thanks and appreciation to my parents, siblings, a host of brothers and sisters in Christ, and an innumerable company of friends and supporters. Your prayers and well wishes are valued greatly. I pray that the love of God will ever resonate in your hearts, minds, and spirits with fervency and power.

About the Author

Dr. Darrell Johnson is Founder and CEO of *Christ the Savior Ministries* a multidimensional evangelical, instructional, and multimedia Christian outreach initiative whose mission is to spread the message of hope, peace, and joy through faithful practice of Christian principles. Additionally, Dr. Johnson is Co-Founder and Director of a private counseling/therapy practice, Compassionate Care Counseling Services.

An ardent believer in the transformative power of education and knowledge, he was conferred the degree of Doctor of Philosophy, Counselor Education from Western Michigan University in 2004. He previously earned a Masters of Arts degree in Counseling in Higher Education from Western Michigan University, a Masters of Education degree in Educational Leadership from Grand Valley State University, a Bachelors of Arts degree in Theology from United Bible College, and a Bachelors of Science degree in Psychology from Michigan State University. In 2003 Dr. Johnson successfully passed the National Counselor Examination and is recognized as a National Certified Counselor by the National Board of Certified Counselors. In

February 2004 he was certified as a fully Licensed Professional Counselor in the State of Michigan.

Dr. Johnson is an avid researcher and writer. In 2002 he authored a self-published book entitled *"A Light in the Darkness"*. He has authored and/or co-authored numerous counseling related articles, and is published in regional and national, refereed journals and publications.

Table of Contents

Acknowledgements

About the Author

Foreword 9

Preface 13

Introduction 17

Chapter 1: Religion, Christianity, and the Human Experience 23

Chapter 2: Our Pursuit for Fulfilling Relationships 35

Chapter 3: The Foundation of Relationship 47

Chapter 4: God-Centered Relationship 57

Chapter 5: "Adam, Where Art Thou?" 71

Chapter 6: A Passion for Relationship 85

Chapter 7: Actions Speak Louder Than Words 105

Chapter 8: The Formula for Relational Freedom 121

Chapter 9: Nurturing the God-Centered Relationship 141

Chapter 10: The Bond Between Relationship and Fulfillment 159

Chapter 11: An Open Invitation 171

Foreword

The Holy Bible is quite arguably the greatest love story known to Man! It chronicles the trials, tribulations and determinate exploits of a forlorn and betrayed lover, Jehovah God. However, in spite of the betrayal by His beloved creation, Man, God's love for humanity withstood the test of time, despair, disappointment and undeniable heartache.

No place are the longing pains of God's love better captured than in the writings of Solomon:

"*I charge you, O daughters of Jerusalem, if ye find my beloved, that ye tell him, that I am sick of love*" (Songs of Solomon 5: 8). [Note: Verses referenced in this book are from the King James Version of the Holy Bible.]

The love of God for humanity endured the agony of incalculable travail. Yet the lovesick overtures of Jehovah God, though invariably rebuffed by the object of His affection, remain undeterred.

Driven by His tenacious inveteracy to be rejoined with His impassioned lost love, God endured the pain of lost and vanquish. No thing, no person, no power, was capable of denying the desire of God to requite His love. Ultimately, through the sacrifice of Jesus Christ, a means whereby the incessant love of God might redound would ultimately be actualized.

The Gospel of Jesus Christ is a declaration of the "good news" that God's love ultimately reigns triumphant. Through the selfless sacrifice of Jesus Christ, the indefatigable love of God is thusly rewarded. God can now be joined with Man again. The sacrifice of Jesus Christ allowed the love of God to be requited and fulfilled once again.

Unfortunately, far too many people fail to realize that the longing desire and void that pervades their heart, mind, and soul can only be satiated by entering into sincere relationship with God through Jesus Christ. *This is the passion of Man!* To be rejoined with the Creator of all life is the only path to true happiness and fulfillment. All other roads only lead to a dead-end street called "Misery"!

The Apostle Paul, speaking of the true nature of charity or love, states:

"(Love) Beareth all things, believeth all things, hopeth all things, endureth all things" (I Corinthians 13: 7).

The love of God for Man has endured for thousand of years. Accordingly, our happiness and fulfillment is inextricably linked to Intimate, sincere relationship with God. The rich splendor of intimacy with God and fullness of joy awaits you. I implore and adjure you to enter into true, intimate relationship with God today! Happiness and fulfillment awaits you!

Preface

"Happy is the man that findeth wisdom, and the man that getteth understanding. For the merchandise of it is better than the merchandise of silver, and the gain thereof than fine gold."

(Proverbs 3: 13-14)

The greatest miracle known to man is a renewed and transformed life, achieved through the power of faith in Jesus Christ! Redemption and eternal relationship with our Creator is the precious gift God grants believers and responders to His earnest call. Jesus Christ made himself a ransom and a substitute on behalf of Mankind. To know Jesus Christ, is to know God, is to know "wisdom"!

Relationship with God through Jesus Christ is **_the passion of Man_**! The consequence of relationship with God is that Christians have been appropriated all rights to what the Apostle Paul refers to as the *"fruits of the Spirit"* (Galatians 5: 22). These include, but are not necessarily limited to joy, peace, love, happiness; and yes, fulfillment. Such is the rich heritage of the Christian faith!

Is your life fulfilling? Does happiness pervade your life? If you are a Christian, is your relationship with God marked with zeal, passion, and exuberance? Do you have a fervent "fire" for the things of God? If you answered "no" to any of these questions, you are living beneath your God-ordained rights and privileges as a follower of Jesus Christ! You must seek to possess the fullness of God's divine promises!

Many people, both Believers and non-Believers are under the misguided notion that Christianity is simply another religion. Nothing can be further from the truth! Christianity is much more than "religion"! Christian faith is about dedicated and religious attentiveness to fostering and nurturing one's "relationship" with God!

It is cute and endearing for individuals in popular culture today to say the words, "you complete me", as an expression of their sincere affections for a companion, spouse, etc. Assuredly, many of these expressions of fondness are grounded in inviolable sincerity. However, our souls, the very essence of life abiding in every human being, can only realize true "completeness" via fervent relationship with God!

This book is a guide for both Christians and inquirers

for negotiating the process of achieving happiness and fulfillment through "God-centered relationship". Perhaps you know God on a superficial level, like a coworker, classmate, neighbor, or colleague. However, God-centered relationship involves knowing God on a much deeper level. God-centered relationship involves attaining true "intimacy" with God!

The passion of Man is relationship with God! Jesus Christ is the pathway! Seek to know God intimately! Then will you be able to say unto God with all sincerity, "you complete me"! God bless you always is my earnest and sincere prayer for you dear friend!

Introduction

Man's quest for a better understanding and knowledge about his origins has been exhaustive. The annals of history are strewn with voluminous attempts to better understand our earthly meaning and purpose. One of our most interminable questions is quite simply, "why am I here?"

Whether or not we acquire an acceptable answer to that simple question can greatly affect our general outlook on and approach to life itself. The incalculable energy expended to resolve this quagmire is beyond comprehension. This book proffers the presentation of a solemn attempt to respond to the above stated question.

In the most basic of terms, our primary meaning and purpose for existence is "relationship"! Relationships are the cornerstones of our earthly existence as human beings! In general, we are social beings by nature. Thus, we are most happy and joyous when we are involved in stable, dependable, consistent, gratifying, and fulfilling relationships. Conversely, misery and despair grips our lives when relational void persists. Too often we are held captive by unstable, undependable, inconsistent, cancerous, and debilitating relationships.

To expand upon this assertion, I would submit that our capacity and wherewithal to engage in fulfilling relationships is a function of our ability to actualize a meaningful and committed "relationship" with God. The awesome, omnipotent, omnipresent, and omniscient God of Glory fashioned Man from the dust of the earth. Man was brought into existence by the mere power of God's word for one purpose. Relationship!

It is the undeniable and ordained will of God that Man, arguably one of His most prized creative Works; willingly choose to be in "relationship" with Him. This fact is clearly borne out by the audacious, unfailing, and indefatigable manner in which God exerted His immeasurable power to facilitate restoration of the relationship He desired to have with humanity.

The culmination of God's ardent pursuit of relationship with Man was realized with the death, burial, resurrection, and ascension of Jesus Christ, the sacrificial Lamb of God. Jesus thereby ushered in the opportunity for

Man to be redeemed from his weary and sin-sick condition! The chance for true relationship with God was purchased through Jesus Christ's submission to the just demands of God. Relationship is now available again for all of Mankind to partake and enjoy.

Loneliness, for any extended period ultimately affects our psychological, emotional, and spiritual wellness. One writer captured the essence of this point when he penned the following profound and prophetic statement; "no man is an island unto himself". To be alone is in direct contradiction to our nature as social beings. In particular, the Holy Bible of the Christian faith denotes the following declaration attributed to God Himself;

*"And the Lord God said, it is not good that the man should be **alone**..."* (Genesis 2: 18).

This verse most notably serves as the foundation and establishment of God's ordained plan for human relationship and the institution of marriage, i.e. the union between the man and woman versions of the human species.

God in His infinite wisdom and understanding of the carnal makeup of the first Man, Adam, provided a "helpmeet" or "complementary partner". More notably, we can clearly surmise from this verse the vital importance God places on relationship for Man, both on a spiritual and natural level.

God's eternal will was/is for human beings to be bonded and connected in relationship. That is because we were created in the "image" and "after the likeness" of God Himself. God is an entity who values relationship. The driving force behind all the creative works of God; light, darkness, the stars, the planets, the known and unknown universes and galaxies, and every living celestial and earthly creature to name a few, is founded upon "relationship"! <u>*Relationship*</u> was God's principal motivation for all of His known and unknown creations!

Consequentially, I would suggest that the undying yearning and seemingly unrequited desire for relationship you've experienced in the past and/or the unrelenting hunger and thirst for relationship you may be experiencing at this very moment is not by happenstance, accident or coincidence. Assuredly, when you were conceived and shaped in your mother's womb, the inclination and desire for relationship was inextricably grafted into the very core of your existence as a living creature. Each and every one of us was born with a passion and desire for relationship!

Relationship is the true "passion" of Man! Relationship, both with God and our human brethren, fosters joy, peace, happiness, and "fulfillment". The aim of this book is to foster a clearer understanding of the significance of possessing a viable, consistent, and fulfilling relationship with God. Be assured that participation in a fulfilling relationship with God is the clearest pathway to human relationships that are more satisfying and fulfilling.

Fervent, effectual, and joyous God-centered relationship is only possible through faithful, deliberate, and steadfast attentiveness. It demands ongoing nurturing. Therefore, daily scriptures and biblically-based salutations are denoted at the end of each chapter. These verses and salutations are designed to aid you with the development of fruit bearing God-centered relationships. By divine authority, I compel the power of the Holy Spirit to enrich your life's God-centered relationships via the prophetic impartations received from these verses and salutations!

I invite and implore every reader of this book to enter into the wonderfully fulfilling sanctuary of "Godly relationship" with zeal and enthusiasm. This is why you were created! This is your purpose and meaning! You deserve it! But more importantly, it is the perfect will of God that you possess it!

Chapter 1

Religion, Christianity, and the Human Experience

The recorded history of Man is evinced with an ongoing search for knowledge and understanding relative to the purpose, reason, and nature of our "existence" or "being". "Why?" has been, and yet remains the basis of a litany of questions for Mankind. People have always, and continue to pose, ponder, and contemplate the "why" of their existence with great angst and toil.

Why am I alive? Why was I born? Why must I die? Why do I exist? The pursuit of satisfactory answers to those and other related queries served as the root of much exploration and investigation undertaken by innumerable scholars. The "why" questions invariably served as the impetus and genesis for such varied disciplines of human inquiry as physics, anthropology, astronomy, astrology, psychology, philosophy, and/or religion just to name a few.

Of the disciplines delineated above, invariably people have looked to the discipline of "religion" in their quest for satisfactory responses to many of those "why" questions. The term "religion" is used in the body of this book to describe the organized embracing of and/or adherence to some form of spiritually based ethos or dogma by self-identified individuals or groups of people. Millions and perhaps billions of people around the world are very likely to acknowledge allegiance to some form of religious faith or doctrine. Consequentially, it would be unwise to dismiss the impact and power of religion on the lives and experiences of the human species.

  Interestingly enough, in spite of overwhelming evidence regarding the significance of religion on the human experience, many "scholars" or those anointed as "intellectuals" often question the veracity of religion as an integral influence on the individual lives of people. The relevance of religion in the landscape of science and other intellectually based inquiry is one of the most disputed and contested issues amongst "learned" scholars. Principally, this is based on the contention of many scholars who suggest that religion fails to meet the standards of rigor associated with "recognized" disciplines of investigation and inquiry.

In particular, the scientific community has historically frowned upon serious consideration of religion as a viable explanation for various problems or issues that may be a focal point of their respective disciplines. In general, scientists offer the argument that the influence of "religious experience" can't be quantifiably measured. Moreover, it is their opinion that religious experiences are subject to variant statistical problems such as poor internal validity and reliability. Finally, they contend that an inability to resolve these latter stated problems may result in erroneous generalizations when attempting to apply religious-based postulates and assertions to the entirety of the human experience.

However, in spite of doubtful disputations by these scholars it is difficult to discount the self-reported impact of religion on the lives of millions/billions of people around the world. One might argue that the sheer number of religious doctrines associated with an almost incalculable number of religious belief systems supports this assertion. It provides a serious challenge to efforts that dismiss the impact of religion and faith in a "higher power" on the human experience.

Moreover, within the context of the religious landscape of the human experience, there is one faith system that has arguably been most influential amongst the many religions pervading the world. It is the Judeo-Christian faith. One would find it extremely difficult to dismiss the influence of the Judeo-Christian faith on the human experience, both historically and contemporarily. It could be argued that the Judeo-Christian faith has been the most important sociopolitical force to affect the course of human history. Inarguably, the impact of the Judeo-Christian faith on the world has been, and continues to be quite quantifiable and measurable.

The Judeo-Christian faith has greatly influenced the manner in which millions of people conduct themselves with respect to their interactions and relationships with other human beings. Historically, the foundations and systems of world governments, wars and conflagrations around the globe, conflicts between various factions within the context of societies and/or cultures, and the uniting of persons from every strata of various countries' milieu can be directly correlated to the influence of the Judeo-Christian faith. Whether or not one agrees with, or embraces the tenets of the Judeo-Christian faith, to refute its significance and importance on the earthly human experience defies all the laws or principles of reason, logic, and scientific discovery.

For adherents or "Believers" of the Judeo-Christian faith, the Holy Bible serves as the cornerstone for understanding and ultimately actualizing the tenets of their faith. For Believers, the Holy Bible is embraced as the "God inspired" delineation of His thoughts. The Holy Bible has become the resolution to the "why" questions for many members of the Man species.

For Believers, the Holy Bible is the most valued, treasured, and life-transforming piece of faith-based literature to have impacted the earthly experience of humanity. The Holy Bible serves as a written record of the thoughts of God relative to His relationship with the Man species. The Holy Bible serves as a treatise between God and Man. It is a detailed declaration of His perspective relative to the form and nature of the "ideal" relationship between God and one of His most treasured creations, Man.

Believers recognize the Holy Bible as the "thoughts"

of God, formally articulated via "inspiration" given to men and women of His choosing. These men and women were God-appointed and God-selected representatives from the Man species. The thoughts of God serve as a summary and history of the human experience within the context of all God's creative works.

These thoughts are based upon one primary and specific objective. The Holy Bible outlines the parameters and conditions whereby the fractured "relationship" between God and Man can be redressed. Parenthetically stated; the Holy Bible articulates God's passionate desire to be in "relationship" with Mankind.

Unfortunately, the relationship between God and Man was fractured and torn asunder by the deeds of the first man, Adam. Nonetheless, God's eternal steadfastness for relationship with Man was undeterred. The misstep of Adam did not catch God unawares or by surprise. The omniscient God of Glory had formulated a plan of action in anticipation of Adam's error. The plan was embodied in the person of God, Jesus Christ.

Thus, the Holy Bible details God's earnest and

passionate desire to be "rejoined" and/or "reconnected" to His prized creation, humanity! As Believers, there is a direct correlation between the status of our relationship with God the Creator and the status of our relationship with Man, the Creation. Fruitful relationship with our fellow man is formed via a wonderfully formed foundation. Reconciliation with God!

Within this foundation Believers find an indefatigable resource for such relationship nurturing ingredients as love, faith, hope, trust, faithfulness, holiness, righteousness, peace, and confidence just to name a few. The sanctity of this glorious reconciliation serves as a baseline that elucidates the manner in which Believers should govern and moderate their interactions with members of the human family.

The aim of this book is to articulate a detailed explanation of the inherent value and benefits of a passionate pursuit of a relationship with God. The byproducts associated with establishing and actively maintaining that relationship is unlimited. Relationship, discipleship, and on-going fellowship with God, are available for all those who will "identify" with the workmanship and sacrifice of Jesus Christ. These are all garnered by participation in the "rebirth" process!

Through rebirth the "just demands" of God are satisfied relative to the "stain of sin" ascribed to every member of the human species at birth. Fortunately, when the rebirth prerequisite has been satisfied, then and only then can true "relationship" occur between God and Man. Unbeknownst to most people, "relationship" is the fervent and ubiquitous desire fundamentally driving most of their actions and deeds during their earthly journey.

"Relationship" is the answer to the "why" questions! Why am I here? God placed you here for "relationship"! Why was I born? God orchestrated your conception and birth into the world for "relationship"! Why am I unhappy? Unfulfilled? Unsatisfied? It is because your "relationship" with God is either nonexistent or only exists superficially at best! As a member of the human family true "relationship" with God is the "only" path to a purposeful and fulfilling earthly existence!

Do you feel that your earthly journey is empty and

replete with disappointment, heartache, and wanton despair? Consider this book is an open invitation to you to evaluate your status and relationship with God. God invites you to engage in a journey as a companion and partner towards God's ordained destiny for you as one of His most beloved Creations! Ask yourself today, why am I living beneath my privilege? What I am allowing to impede my path to the richness of joy and satisfaction God proffers to those who look to Him for respite from the ravages and toils of a degraded world?

If you have not already done so, I implore you to surrender yourself to the indomitable and indefatigable love of God. Allow God's soothing touch to penetrate your heart, mind, and soul by identifying with the supremely demonstrated and magnanimous sacrifice of Jesus Christ. It is God's passionate desire to "tabernacle" with you today!

Allowing God to take up residence in your heart and soul will assuredly do you well. Possession of this stupendous privilege from God is both attainable and sustainable. It is God's longing desire for Mankind. Choose today to enter into true relationship with Him! Jesus Christ is the pathway! An innumerable company of witnesses can attest that it is the one decision in your life for which you shall be eternally grateful! In doing so, be assured that the true passion of your life, fervent relationship with God, will become a reality!

Daily Verses & Salutations

"I will bless the Lord at all times: his praise shall continually be in my mouth". (Psalms 34: 1)

"My soul shall make her boast in the LORD: the humble shall hear [thereof], and be glad." (Psalms 34: 2)

"[I had fainted], unless I had believed to see the goodness of the LORD in the land of the living." (Psalms 27: 13)

"Blessed [is the man whom] thou choosest, and causest to approach [unto thee, that] he may dwell in thy courts: we shall be satisfied with the goodness of thy house, [even] of thy holy temple." (Psalms 65: 4)

Dear Lord, I give you myself wholly and completely. I honor you with the fruit of my lips, with my thoughts, with my desires, and with my daily intents.

Dear Lord, I am so proud to have you in my life! I will never be ashamed of you! My hearts desire is to tell the world how wonderfully great and awesome you are!

My God, my God! When I think of the goodness of Jesus, and all He has done for me, MY SOUL cries out, Hallejuah, **<u>THANK GOD FOR SAVING ME!!!!</u>**

Notes, Reflections, and Revelations

Chapter 2

<u>Our Pursuit for Fulfilling Relationships</u>

The canon of the Christian faith, the "Holy Bible", outlines the meticulous and fastidious extent of God's desire for a faithful, committed relationship with one of His most precious creations; humanity. Similarly, our entire earthly existence is principally focused on the dogged pursuit to fulfill our intrinsic drive to be connected to another. This drive for "connectedness" is often beyond the realm of understanding of most people.

All too often we are oblivious to our drive for connectedness, at least on a conscious level. However, it resides and percolates deep within the recesses and core of our individual souls! We typically have a "gut feeling" that no matter how many material possessions we accumulate, power and prestige we garner from humanity, and/or other means we accrue to satisfy our carnal desires, a void persists.

Our efforts to subjugate the yearning and emptiness residing within our soul breeds frustration and anguish.

Resolution of our plight seems futile! We seem incapable and helpless when it comes to appeasing the need for connectedness. Until the "relationship" void is filled, a sense of incompleteness persists in our lives.

Without "relationship", we exist in the obscure vacuum of a lonely, solitary, and isolated world called "the mind". The mind demands the fruit of relationship and connection. With connectedness, the mind is an inveterate place of solace and refuge. With absence of connectedness, the mind is an interminable residence of despair.

Either way, we can never escape the mind. Without relationship, the mind is a vast and unceasingly boring terrain. Thus, our earthly existence is like an expedition in search of golden nuggets of companionship and connectedness. For many people, those golden nuggets appear to be mined away in a remote, barren and vast wasteland. The inability to retrieve those golden nuggets breeds frustration and heartache for prospectors of those nuggets.

During our earthly journey, we strive to locate visceral landmarks denoting the poignant occasions of connectedness. These exquisitely laden mental, emotional, and/or spiritual experiences provide us with a strong sense of relevance and validation. Possessions only provide us momentary and fleeting satisfaction!

Accumulated wealth is a wonderful thing! But only sincere, devoted, and committed relationship can fill the lingering emptiness, often presiding over our earthly existence. Where there is relationship, there is hope! Where there is relationship, there is purpose! Where there is relationship, there is peace!

For Christians, the Holy Bible provides a succinct illustration of God as the paragon of true relationship. How so? Prior to the existence of humanity, there was God. Prior to the existence of the celestial creatures, there was God. God's existence was solitary. Nothing else existed. Only God! Our finite minds do not possess the capacity to comprehend or fathom the concept of "nothing"!

The absence of all things that now occupy the known and unknown world(s), solar system(s), universe(s), and galaxy(s), encapsulates the essence of God's "pre-creation" existence. Nothing and no one was physically or spiritually present with whom God could interact. At some point however, somewhere in the great expanse of God's mind and thoughts, "interaction" ostensibly became a relevant and pertinent issue. Herein was the concept of "relationship" constructed. Accordingly, God chose to create other beings or entities with whom He might find "connectedness" and "relationship".

As intimated previously, a paucity of information is at our disposal which provides complete details regarding the creative works of God (e.g., the heavens, the solar system, Earth, celestial and earthly creatures) and the inception of time. Whatever the reason, God apparently chose to create or "speak into existence" celestial beings, presumably for the purpose of initiating His first phase of the "relationship" experiment. Likewise, all of the animals and other earthly creatures God spoke into existence after forming the Earth predate Man's existence based on the record of Genesis 1 & 2 in the Holy Bible.

However, in Man God established a unique phase of "relationship". It appears to supersede the connection God has with other celestial and/or earthly creatures. Man was created in the image of God. In Man resides the capacity for thought, reasoning, logic, and perhaps most importantly, "free will" or choice. Man possesses a "soul". While we do not know the exact composition of the soul, whether it is tangible or intangible, the Bible clearly indicates that the soul is eternal and enduring.

Notably, the soul functions as a "conduit" or connection between God and Man. Granted, our physical body is conceived from the joining of our earthly father's sperm and an egg from our mother's ovum. We all received two strands of deoxyribonucleic acid (DNA) from our respective parents, each with their complement of 23 chromosomes. The body we ultimately inhabit was constructed via the replication of billions of cells during the 36 week (or thereabouts) gestation period preceding our birth. Human birth is truly a wondrous miracle!

But just as miraculously, our bodies would not become "living vessels" until the awesome authority and workmanship of the eternal and all wise "Architect" completes the process. It is not until God deposits the "soul" in the fetus developing in our mother's womb that we truly become a "living soul"! It is the God activated soul of Man that earnestly desires to be in "relationship" with its Heavenly Father, God Almighty!

It is not abundantly clear where Man fits in the hierarchy of all of God's creative works and wonders. Nonetheless, what is irrefutably evident is that God ascribes a high premium on His relationship with Man. This assertion is supported by the expression of God's love for Man. This love is demonstrated by the extreme lengths that God has extended Himself in an attempt to reconcile the schism (caused by the "sin" condition) between God and Man. John stated it best in perhaps the most well-known verse in the Holy Bible:

"For God so loved the world, that he gave His only begotten Son, that whosoever believeth in him should not perish, but have everlasting life" (John 3: 16)

The "life" of which Saint John refers is more fundamentally defined as "eternal fellowship and communion" with God. Every soul exists eternally. Like matter, our soul is never truly destroyed or obliterated, at least as we understand those concepts. Granted, our earthly body shall one day return to the dust of the earth from whence it came.

But the soul continues on. It shall have eternal residence in either one of two places. Glorious habitation with God, or utterly horrendous habitation in the Lake of Fire! Upon receipt and understanding of this information, each of us must make a decision that bears far reaching repercussions and consequences!

Thus emerged the purpose and mission of Jesus Christ. To fulfill God's incessant desire to reconnect with humanity! In the personhood of Jesus Christ, God clothed Himself in a veil of human flesh. Jesus took on the mantle of humanity to rescue His beloved creation, Man.

Jesus purchased our salvation in response to the just demands of God. Before the foundation of the world, before time began, God desired to be in relationship with us. Similarly, while the vast majority of the human race is oblivious of this fact, the fervent desire of our individual souls is to be in relationship with our Creator, God, and Savior.

As we come to better understand the critical value God places on relationship, accordingly, are we then able to thoroughly appreciate the vital role and significance of our human relationships. The quality of our earthly journey is a direct function of whether or not we can nurture positive and productive God-centered human relationships. "God-centered" relationship shall be elucidated in greater depth at a later juncture of the book.

In my experience as a psychotherapist and Christian counselor, I've encountered many people who've had inordinately troubled and challenging life experiences. Generally those individuals tend to have a limited ability to foster productive and fruitful human relationships. Moreover, even people who might be described as well functioning and adept at interpersonal relations will admit to the occasional relational conflict.

We can all attest (or confess) to occasions when even our most treasured relationships are strained and sometimes decimated. Disagreements, arguments, differences of opinions, selfishness, and other factors can obliterate marriages, friendships, and familial relations. God must reside in the center of all our human relationships if they are to be productive, constructive, and fulfilling!

The Word of God is a relational development, enhancement, and maintenance instruction manual. It offers us a model, developed and tested by God, to pattern all of our human relationships. Such fundamental principles as liberality, humility, patience, longsuffering, and self-denial are attributes illustrated within the *"volume of the book"* intended to guide us in the maintenance and support of our human relationships.

But the most notable attribute *"agape love"*, an extension or byproduct of the influence of the Spirit of God, is what we must embrace, emulate, and practice in order to foster loving, productive, and fruitful human relationships. When we inculcate and actively practice the principles outlined in the hallowed Word of God, our entire earthly experience is improved exponentially. We experience joy and fulfillment much more consistently in our daily life.

Our earthly journey is richer and fuller. And if that were not enough, we have a promise and covenant with God ensuring a splendiferous eternal existence. Who could ask for more? Glory to God!

Daily Verses & Salutations

"Thine, O LORD, is the greatness, and the power, and the glory, and the victory, and the majesty: for all [that] is in the heaven and in the earth [is thine]; thine [is] the kingdom, O LORD, and thou art exalted as head above all."(1 Chronicles 29: 11)

"Honour and majesty [are] before him: strength and beauty [are] in his sanctuary." (Psalms 96: 6)

"Bless the LORD, O my soul. O LORD my God, thou art very great; thou art clothed with honour and majesty." (Psalms 104: 1)

"I will speak of the glorious honour of thy majesty, and of thy wondrous works." (Psalms 145: 5)

My dearest Lord & Savior, there is none like you. You are the greatest! You are all powerful! You are majestic! I honor and extol you for your greatness! I give complete and total control of my life to you!

Notes, Reflections, and Revelations

Chapter 3

The Foundation of Relationship

God's relationship with Man is simultaneously an interesting and paradoxical phenomenon. This is especially true when we consider the context in which this relationship was established and founded. Our knowledge of God's existence, activities and interactions prior to His dealings with humanity are vague at best. We know very little about the "eternity-past" experiences of God. We only have the minor clues God has chosen to share with us through His written Word (*Greek- logos, the thoughts of God*).

The initial history of God's relationship with humanity was imparted to Moses and delineated as a reference for generations to come in the Book of Genesis of the Holy Bible. Therein we find in the first clause, of the first verse, of the first chapter of Genesis (also known as the book of the beginnings) the first clue about the experience of the pre-humanity God. It reads as follows: *"In the beginning God..."*. Based on this clause we can deduce several things.

First, before there was a "beginning", God was. In

essence, God's existence predates "time" itself. Secondly, the Bible informs us that it was God who created the very concept of "time". "Time" was introduced as a system of measurement for the dispensation of the earthly human experience. Time revolves around the cycle of our solar system. Moses indicates *"And the evening and the morning were the first day"*. Finally, prior to the inception of humanity, "time" was a non-existent and essentially unnecessary concept in the commonwealth of God.

The "beginning" refers to the initiation of God's creative work leading to humanity's existence. The Holy Bible also declares to us that God (as we know Him) "always was". He had no beginning and shall have no ending! Note Revelation 1: 8:

"I am Alpha and Omega, the beginning and the ending, saith the Lord, which is, and which was, and which is to come, the Almighty."

Being sovereign and providential, God did not require consultation or counsel from any other entity. His "good pleasure" and will are irrefutable!

God resides in eternity. He is not bound by time, space, or any other physical limitation. All power is at His disposal. Thus, the impetus and motivation for creating humanity would certainly evoke one of the "why" questions. Clearly, one might presume that the very presence of the entirety of heavenly hosts and celestial beings (angels) would aptly serve as a source of relationship for God should He desire the same.

From what we can deduce from the Scriptures, the heavenly hosts were/are at the disposal of God the Almighty to worship Him and attend to His every beckoning call. We see varying instances in which angels have been dispatched at the insistence and behest of God to intervene in the affairs of humanity. Angels (Gabriel and Michael are angels who've been designated by a specific name) have served as messengers (see Genesis 19: 1, John 20: 12, Revelation 7:2) and as warriors/combatants (see I Chronicles 21: 12, 15, 30; Isaiah 37: 36; Daniel 6: 22; Revelations 9: 18; 12: 1-9) at the behest of God the Almighty. Lucifer, prior to his excommunication from Heaven (see Isaiah 14: 12; and

Revelations 12: 1-9) with a third of heaven's angels, we can deduce by various inferences in the Scriptures served in the capacity of Chief Musician of the heavenly hosts.

We possess little knowledge of the history and pre-humanity activities or interactions between God and His angels. However, it is clear that God was not particularly in need of other beings or entities for the purpose of relationship. Given the fact God had angels at His ready disposal in the event He so desired relationship, why did He choose to create Man? What was God's motivation for creating Man when he had the entirety of the heavenly host with whom to interact?

David, a man with whom God had a vast amount of involvement and interaction pondered some iteration of these latter mentioned questions, often to great painstaking lengths. This is quite evident when we consider a body of prose, much of which is consider some of David's most profound, poignant, popular and widely recognized writings, the Book of Psalms. In particular, take note to Psalms 8: 3-4:

"When I consider thy heavens, the work of thy fingers, the moon and the stars, which thou hast ordained, What is man, that thou art mindful of him? And the son of man **(Jesus Christ)**, *that thou visitest him?"*

Likewise consider these words uttered by David relative to God's mindfulness of man:

"Many, O LORD my God, are thy wonderful works which thou hast done, and thy thoughts which are to us-ward: they cannot be reckoned up in order unto thee: if I would declare and speak of them, they are more than can be numbered." (Psalms 40: 5)

The notion that God would even be bothered with or concern Himself with Man is beyond comprehension. God had the entirety of the heavenly host (angels) at His disposal of which He could be in relationship. What was/is it about man that God would be "mindful" of us? Consider as well the distinction between men and angels.

Both men and angels possess a free will or volition. Men, however, were created from the matter of the Earth.

Thus, we are distinguished from angels at our inception when we are assigned a physical (earth-based) body and a soul! We have little information relative to God's reasoning and motive for shaping and fashioning us in this manner. However, there is one very plausible explanation. Glory!

Consider the susceptibility and predisposition of our physical (carnal) makeup. The flesh inclines itself towards seemingly undeterred self-gratification and appeasement. The Apostle Paul suggests that our flesh is likened unto a ravenous beast. Our earthly "temples" or houses have one primary passionate objective, to be satisfied. The flesh is voracious and unrelenting. Lust, pride, self-will, and outright defiance are the byproducts of an unrestrained carnal nature. The unabated carnal nature of man drives him to inordinate lengths to satiate its appetite. Often to the point of debilitation, incapacity, and ultimately, utter destruction!

It is in the context of this seemingly inveterate and hopeless condition that God envisioned an opportunity to appropriate glory for Himself. Thus was humanity's purpose conceived! Consider the magnanimous glory afforded God when His creation, Man, chooses of his own accord to worship, extol, magnify, and honor Him, in the midst of the unceasing demands of corruptible flesh.

The makeup of our earthly tabernacle compels us to negotiate with this ubiquitous and persistent demand for gratification. Thus, we struggle with a continuous internal conflict. Our choice has grave repercussions. If we choose to wholly submit to our fleshly desires, we can expect the discord of a troubled soul destined for eternal agony and the despair of isolation from God. Conversely, if we choose to subjugate the inordinate passions of our flesh, we obtain peace for our soul via a wondrously, inconceivable eternal relationship in the company of God.

Imagine the loving glory and honor experienced by God when a woman, man, girl or boy chooses the latter of the two options above of their own volition and free will. Choosing God in the face of the unceasing pressures to satisfy our carnal desires assuredly brightens the countenance of God. Our __*choice*__ is tantamount to glorifying God. Surely God is well pleased with all those who've made a conscious and calculated choice of Him!

Therefore, in the most basic of terms, making a

decision about the basis of our eternal relationship with God is the dilemma we all must resolve throughout our earthly journey. Contemplate all of the power and authority at the disposal of God. The vastness of His reach and capabilities are beyond our comprehension and understanding. Yet God "chose" to expend the power of His creative mind and thoughts to orchestrate the creation of Man for one primary purpose. "Relationship"!

Oh, what a marvelous opportunity and privilege we have been granted by God. How can we neglect such an awesome and precious opportunity? If you have not already done so, I implore you to consider God. Choose wisely. The benefits and rewards of relationship with God far outweigh the presumed costs of the same!

Daily Verses & Salutations

"The God of my rock; in him will I trust: [he] is my shield, and the horn of my salvation, my high tower, and my refuge, my saviour; thou savest me from violence." (2 Samuel 22: 3)

"[As for God], his way is perfect; the word of the LORD [is] tried: he [is] a buckler to all them that trust in him." (2 Samuel 22: 31)

"I will say of the LORD, [He is] my refuge and my fortress: my God; in him will I trust." (Psalms 91: 2)

"Trust in the LORD with all thine heart; and lean not unto thine own understanding." (Proverbs 3: 5)

"Every word of God [is] pure: he [is] a shield unto them that put their trust in him." (Proverbs 30: 5)

"Behold, God [is] my salvation; I will trust, and not be afraid: for the LORD JEHOVAH is my strength and my song; he also is become my salvation." (Isaiah 12: 2)

Dear God, thank you for being dependable and faithful! Cast away all fear and doubt from my mind and heart! Teach me how to lean and depend on you, totally and completely! I will trust you with my life, my hopes, and my dreams!

Notes, Reflections, and Revelations

Chapter 4

God-Centered Relationship

The primary intent of the preceding chapters of this book was to establish a basic understanding relative to the biblical foundation for relationship. Clearly the Scriptures support the thesis that relationship is a predominant focus of our earthly and eternal existence. However, at this point I think it imperative to engage in a discussion about the concept of relationship in a more definitive manner. Let us now take time to give more consideration to the nature and character of what I call the "God-centered relationship".

A God-centered relationship exceeds the typical perception and/or manner for dealing with God. It transcends the scope of "superficial" forms of relatedness exemplified in a majority of the human relationships we've developed and grown accustomed to in our everyday lives. A God-centered relationship is founded upon an understanding between two amenable parties, who've committed themselves to an eternally felicitous covenant.

Unlike many of our human relationships, the God-centered relationship consists of something far more intense than a mere fleeting and passing moment of interest. It is much more dependable than the close bond you might have with a lifelong friend. The God-centered relationship does not resemble the connection you have with a close associate, an acquaintance, a colleague, a confidant, or a business partner. In fact, the God-ordained bond between a husband and wife, accompanied by fervent love, passion and marital bliss sustaining is a mere close facsimile of the kind of union God aspires to have with us.

The God-centered relationship is established when we willingly heed the beckoning and call to our souls by God to be intimately joined with Him. The call and pull of God upon our souls begins with our inception into the earthly realm. The pull of God comes in the form of His Spirit drawing on the cords and strings of our individual hearts. David aptly describes the inveterate call of God as follows:

"Deep calleth unto deep at the noise of thy waterspouts: all thy waves and thy billows are gone over me."
(Psalms 42: 7)

The verse above conveys the thought that God engages in a concerted effort to reach out to each of us. Liken unto a zealous suitor, desirous of the affections and attention of the "apple of his/her eye", God is willing to exercise all of His power in pursuit of us. David metaphorically describes God's use of the very elements of the earth to assuage and appeal to us. God's goes to such great lengths to achieve something far greater than a cursory connection with us. His desires is that our soul, our essence, be "joined" again with the source from which it came; the Eternal Spirit of God!

One would be greatly challenged to find any other literary prose besides the Song of Solomon that eloquently and adroitly illustrates God's fervent love and concern for His Beloved, His "Bride"! The Bride is the Church of the Living God. Inarguably, the Church, in a corporate sense, is the focus of God's affection. However, by extrapolation, this affection is also extended to us individually.

The allegorical nature of the Song of Solomon was penned to describe the kind of love upon which a God-centered relationship is founded. Solomon does this with tedious and immaculate lucidity. The beauty and eloquent nature of his God-inspired prose is almost intoxicating. Such is the nature of a God-centered relationship!

The Song of Solomon articulates the experience of a forlorn Shumanite woman, who becomes enraptured with her desire for the affections of a shepherd boy. However, circumstances preclude her from realizing the longing ambition and love of her intoxicated heart to be joined with the object of her affection. She retorts concerning her despair and disappointment at the notice of the departure and absence of her suitor as such:

"Let him kiss me with the kisses of his mouth: for thy love is better than wine". (Song of Solomon 1: 2)

In Chapter 2: 8-9 the depth of her longing, the fervency of her desire, and warm, glowing aroma of her affection is elucidated:

"The voice of my beloved! behold, he cometh leaping upon the mountains, skipping upon the hills. My beloved is like a roe or a young hart: behold, he standeth behind our wall, he looketh forth at

the windows, shewing himself through the lattice."

With a rebuffed and unrequited heart, she adamantly seeks to be rejoined with her beloved. Metaphorically she makes constant and unabated inquiries of Solomon and others concerning the location of her hoped for suitor. Solomon writes:

"By night on my bed I sought him whom my soul loveth: I sought him, but I found him not. I will rise now, and go about the city in the streets, and in the broad ways I will seek him whom my soul loveth: I sought him, but I found him not. The watchmen that go about the city found me: [to whom] I [said], Saw ye him whom my soul loveth?" (Song of Solomon 3: 1-3)

In the interim, she abides and waits with baited breath and anticipation of the return of her beloved. Approached and appealed to by other potential suitors, she remains loyal and steadfast to the commitment she has fortified in her heart for the wayward shepherd. Although undeterred in her mission to be rejoined with her beloved, understandably, she is pained by the prolonged delay in his arrival. Solomon states:

"I charge you, O daughters of Jerusalem, if ye find my beloved, that ye tell him, that I [am] sick of love." (Song of Solomon 5: 8)

But alas, after a long and laborious journey, the Shumanite maiden ultimately realizes her goal. Her beloved finally returns to her. Her wanton desire has been fulfilled. She is ecstatic and relieved. Finally, her joy is complete! She has been rejoined with the one for whom her heart ached and longed for.

The allegory of the Shumanite maiden is exhilarating to those who are true romanticists. It provides us with a poignant glimpse of the energy God exercised in pursuit of His Bride, the Church. The wonderful imagery of the Song describes a forlorn admirer, who musters an unimaginable amount of fortitude, restraint, and determination, bent on one day realizing her/his dream.

The Song of Solomon mirrors so many unending searches for love and companionship. Untold numbers of people around the globe can attest to a personal journey through seemingly vehement and disparaging storms, in search of an unrequited love. It is the stuff great novels, love songs, and motion pictures are derived from.

The Song of Solomon is a lucid literary representation of the experience of God with humanity. It mirrors God's fastidious and undeterred drive to actualize His fundamental motive for creating the species of humanity. Relationship! In so many respects, God has pursued relationship with humanity with the same vigor exhibited by the Shumanite maiden for her shepherd. In the possible event you've been the object of affection of an admirer, you probably have a nominal point of reference to appreciate the significance of the allegory.

Presuming you've been sought after by a man or woman, or conversely, acted in the role of ardent pursuer of another, you may possess a small measure of understanding of what God has experienced with humanity. Innumerable accounts exist from people who've endured sleepless nights, diminished or lost appetites, an inability to concentrate on the most insignificant of tasks and aching hearts. All of which they will likely attribute to the unwillingness of someone to requite of them of their longing love and affection. Such is the plight of those who dare to flirt with the splendor and at times, travails of love and relationship.

Nonetheless, I would contend that any vanquished tryst we've experienced, no matter how disheartening and emotionally lurid is minuscule in comparison to what God has endured. Consider this. Take a moment to reflect upon your current relational status with God. Do you have a truly committed relationship with Him? If not, what doth hinder you? What impedes your ability to acquiesce and surrender to His overtures? Why do you allow temporal things, desires, and/or people to interfere with your eternal fidelity with God?

If you consider yourself to be in good standing and relationship with God, reflect on the conditions by which He was finally able to consummate the union (spiritual regeneration) between the two of you. Since the day you were reconciled with God, can you honestly say that you've passionately sought to fortify your relationship with Him? Are you continuing to pursue God with vigor, fervor, and zeal? Is your relational passion for God foment and intense or flaccid and lukewarm?

In summation, the intent of this section of the book is to elucidate the true nature of the God-centered relationship. The most distinguishing quality of this type of relationship is its stability and durability. It is founded upon mutually embraced and practiced characteristics as trust, faith, faithfulness, consistency, attentiveness, caring, gentleness, and firmness. Not surprising is the fact that both your relationship with God and humanity are more likely to be fruitful, fulfilling, and satisfying if and when you make a concerted effort to embrace and inculcate this litany of characteristics.

The sense of dependability endemic to God-centered relationship tends to foster a calming and soothing balm of security for the relational partners. Whether divine or human, the recipient will liken the experience (like that of the Shumanite maiden) to being enveloped in a euphoric swirl of loving concern and affection. Driven by the desire to be a continual recipient of the affection, one can't help but be compelled to reciprocate, over and over and over again.

Both members of this resplendent union become enraptured in a symphony of never-ending zeal to reciprocate the inebriating affection of the other. Exhaustion is but a tepid concern for the parties of this type of union. Only the continuation of rapturous joy, satisfaction, and fulfillment of the other truly matters. For in the process of satiating the desires of one's partner, one's own effort to fortify the relationship will redound with concomitant ferocity and intensity.

As the beloved of God, you have the assurance of being the single focal point of His concern, even within the context of incalculable numbers of celestial and earthly beings. For God is so magnanimous that He possesses the ability to simultaneously manage the activity and continuity of all the known and unknown worlds and yet remain attentive to your unique concerns, desires, and needs. Your wellness is His stolid and resolute preoccupation!

In the midst of an innumerable company of celestial beings, billions of human beings, and perhaps trillions and quadrillions of other earthly creatures, God has the wherewithal and will to focus his attention to your every whim. What an awesome and marvelous God! Who could ask for anything more in a devoted and faithful companion?

In the words of a profound and enduring hymn, "If I had ten thousand tongues, I wouldn't be able to praise Him enough, for all He's done for me!" I don't know about you, but my life's determination was illustriously captured in the words of Joshua when he queried and admonished the people of God with respect to their allegiance:

> "*...but as for me and my house, we will serve the Lord*".
> (Joshua 24: 15)

When you thoroughly consider the wonderful benefits of serving God, there is really no choice at all. God gets my vote! Selah!

Daily Verses & Salutations

"Let him kiss me with the kisses of his mouth: for thy love is better than wine." (Song of Solomon 1: 2)

"Thy cheeks are comely with rows [of jewels], thy neck with chains [of gold]." (Song of Solomon 1: 10)

"Behold, thou [art] fair, my love; behold, thou [art] fair; thou [hast] doves' eyes." (Song of Solomon 1: 15)

"He brought me to the banqueting house, and his banner over me was love." (Song of Solomon 2: 4)

"O my dove, [that art] in the clefts of the rock, in the secret [places] of the stairs, let me see thy countenance, let me hear thy voice; for sweet [is] thy voice, and thy countenance [is] comely." (Song of Solomon 2: 14)

Dearest God, I get excited when I think about you! Your joy, is my joy! Your desire, is my desire! I blow kisses to you God! You make my heart race! You are the best thing that ever happened to ME!

Notes, Reflections, and Revelations

Chapter 5

"Adam, Where Art Thou?"

Relationship between God the Creator and Man the Creation has always been of paramount concern. As suggested in earlier portions of this book, relationship was/is the very basis for which Man was brought into existence. Relationship was/is the imperative that influenced God to lend His sovereign power to the procurement of Man's redemption.

Through Jesus, we are able to be a part of the commonwealth of God's Eternal Kingdom. In literal terms, God demonstrated a passionate interest in relationship with Man. He made provision for that relationship in the person of Jesus Christ. His sacrificial work at Calvary provided for the redemption of all our fallen and spiritually decrepit souls.

What was it that necessitated the demand for the sinless blood of Jesus Christ to atone for the sins of all Humanity? Stated simply, it was/is the lack of attention to and appreciation for the basic requirements God demands to sustain a truly viable relationship with Him. Adam, who represented the first Man to be in relationship with God, knowingly chose to ignore the simplest of laws mandated by God. Note the following:

"And the Lord God commanded the man, saying, Of every tree of the garden thou mayest freely eat; But of the tree of the knowledge of good and evil, thou shalt not eat of it:…"
(Genesis 2: 16 & 17a, b)

Adam was granted the splendorous opportunity to eternally reside in the glorious state of relationship with God. The wonder of this outstanding opportunity could only be fully appreciated when one considers the simplistic nature of the condition by which it was predicated. Consider that Adam had his every need provided for in the Garden of Eden. Adam could liberally enjoy the innumerable benefits of residing in an indescribably glorious garden, where his every whim, desire, and need would be provided for.

Adam could incessantly bask in the warmth, beauty, and undoubtedly indescribable ebullience of communion with his Creator in the Garden of Eden. Adam had the assurance of God that no concern for the provision of life-sustaining sustenance would be necessary to allow him to live eternally. So what was the one condition that God prevailed upon Adam to ensure the fortification of those promises from God? Do not partake of the one tree that would forever eviscerate the innocence of Adam with respect to his conception of what is good and evil, right and wrong.

So what was the penalty for disobedience? The latter clause of Genesis 2: 17 clearly highlights the seriousness of such an act:

"...for in the day that thou eatest thereof thou shalt surely die".

Adam could not possibly have fully understood nor appreciate the gravity of his decision to neglect the simple mandate of God. Likewise, today it is imperative that we make a concerted effort to absorb the significance of this clause, both for Adam and for all humanity. Parenthetically stated, this declaration by God would serve as the introduction of what heretofore was very likely a foreign, mysterious and somewhat incomprehensible concept. Quite simply, would to know the concept of "death".

A paucity of information exists (the record delineated by Moses in the Book of Genesis is the only real source of information at our disposal) relative to the length of time and complete nature of the relationship between God and Adam. Thus, we can only deduce from the Scriptures that the relationship between God and Adam was active, fruitful, and consistent. Adam could depend on God to "visit" him with His "presence" on a regular basis. Note Genesis 3: 8:

"And they heard the voice of the Lord God walking in the garden in the cool of the day,…"

Presumably, the visitation between God and Adam consisted of something more than the ebullience of God's presence upon the visage of Adam (and later Eve). Evidently, the visitation also entailed audible communication or "communion" between God and Adam. This assertion is validated in the previously stated verse

(Genesis 2:16) wherein God orally instructed Adam (*"And the Lord God commanded the man, **saying**..."*) regarding the conditions for fortifying his continuous status as a resident of the Garden.

Likewise, in Genesis 3: 8, Moses indicates that Adam and Eve *"**heard** the voice of the Lord"*. The critical value and importance of ongoing "communion" with God by contemporary believers will be addressed in greater depth in a later section of this book. It is impossible to commune with God in absence of true relationship. It is impossible to hear from God in the absence of true relationship. God-centered relationship activates the "spiritual antenna" of our heart and soul! God-centered relationship unscrambles, crystallizes, and individually encrypts communication between God and man.

So what is the significance of highlighting the concepts of visitation and communion between God and Adam? These issues were precursors of the principal long-term interest God would have with Man. "Relationship!" The emphasis God ascribes to the initial relationship between Him and Adam is quite notable given the fact

Moses was inspired (Paul informs us that *"all scripture is given by inspiration of God,..."*) to delineate the nature of their relationship at the beginning of the Book of Beginnings (Genesis).

Genesis serves as the cornerstone of God's intentions with respect to His original plan for humanity. The workmanship of Jesus Christ garnered the possibility for contemporary believers to fulfill God's original plan for humanity. Paul indicates in Ephesians 1: 11 that because of Christ:

*"...we have obtained an inheritance, being **predestinated** according to the purpose of him who worketh all things after the counsel of his own will:...".*

Therefore, because of Jesus Christ, God's plan for viable relationship with humanity could once again become a reality for incalculable numbers of future generations of believers.

At this juncture, I would like to take a moment to allot space for more in-depth consideration of a concept introduced earlier in this chapter, "death". I would posit that the primary reason that men and women dismiss, neglect, and/or ignore the Gospel message is directly related to their lack of understanding of the concept of death. A rudimentary definition of death is the "termination of life". Another definition is "the end or extinction of one's existence".

However, God has a somewhat different version of what "death" means for humanity. It is literally the eternal separation of Man from his life force, God. It involves complete and total disconnection between Man's life essence, the soul, and God the Creator. It is a place of unknowing loneliness and utter despair. It is a place of eternal misery and agony. Death consists of complete awareness and consciousness of one's existence, yet simultaneously being unable to touch, feel, or be in fellowship with Him who gives meaning and purpose for existing. Death is a total absence of "relationship" with God!

Of course, to those who don't know God through the "new-birth" experience in effect their present lives represents a form of the aforestated concept of "death".

Absence of a true relationship with God is tantamount to separation from God. However, the Bible emphatically declares that even if our physical bodies were to perish or die, there is yet another death (eternal separation of the soul from God) to be concerned about.

In Genesis 3: 9, God posed a question to Adam which has incredible significance for every human that would follow after him. The verse states:

"And the Lord God called unto Adam, and said unto him, Where art thou?"

Indisputably, the omniscient God of Glory was fully aware of the physical location of Adam. The essence of His query was activated by God's recognition that the "bond" or "relationship" between He and Adam had been aborted and severed.

As Adam began to consume the forbidden fruit, his brain activated the release of vital digestive enzymes via his saliva. This initiated the food digestive process. A signal was transmitted to God. What God had known and anticipated would occur before the foundations of the world, had come to fruition.

Thus, the inquisition from God; *"Adam"* (my beloved, my treasure, my dearest creature*)*, *"where art thou"*? The phrase *"where art thou?"* might be better transliterated to say, "Why have you instigated this rift between us? I (God) detect that the soundness of our bond, our connection, our 'relationship' has been torn asunder".

As a mother hen broods over her chicks, so watched God over Adam and Eve. The love God had for Adam and Eve is beyond our comprehension. He fawned over Man as a proud parent over a newborn child. And in the same manner that a mother or father would undoubtedly be consumed and stricken with untold fear and agony over the incredulous possibility her/his child has been kidnapped or worse, killed, God experienced the same with the fall of Adam and Eve.

Sin and accordingly, death, became the reality of Adam's (and Eve's) earthly experience. Consequentially, the rift between God and Adam was transferred to every person born into this world. David elucidates the predicament which befell all humanity because of Adam's transgression in the following verse:

> "Behold, I was shapen in iniquity; and in sin did my mother conceive me". (Psalms 51: 5)

In spite of Adam's failure, God's passionate desire for relationship was unrelenting. God stolidly refused to accept the fate of Man and surrender His creation without expending effort to retain this valued relationship. Anticipating the surreptitious and nefarious act of Satan to subjugate Man, God, in His infinite wisdom instituted a plan before time itself came into existence. Jesus Christ would serve as the mediator between God and Man. John, referring to Jesus Christ declares:

> "...the Lamb slain from the foundation of the world" (Revelation 13: 8).

Unfortunately, our finite minds are incapable of conceiving the sheer gravity and horror of eternal separation from God. Fortunately, as long as you have breath in your body, and the ability to exercise faith towards God, you have an opportunity to be reconciled with God. If you don't know God in the pardon of your sins, please incline your ear to hear the call of God. God is seeking you with fervent desire. God is calling you today! *Where art thou* _____*(insert your name here)*_____?

The pathway back to the suitor of your soul and the arbiter of your eternal habitation is easy to locate. Jesus Christ paved the eternal freeway to Glory. It only requires the most basic of effort on your part. Faith in the workmanship of Jesus Christ at Calvary, coupled with completion of the new-birth process affords one the privilege of avoiding eternal separation from God. I adjure you; seek God while He may be found. Eternity with God awaits you!

Daily Verses & Salutations

"But if from thence thou shalt seek the LORD thy God, thou shalt find [him], if thou seek him with all thy heart and with all thy soul." (Deuteronomy 4: 29)

"Glory ye in his holy name: let the heart of them rejoice that seek the LORD." (1 Chronicles 16: 10)

"The young lions do lack, and suffer hunger: but they that seek the LORD shall not want any good [thing]." (Psalms 34: 10)

"Sow to yourselves in righteousness, reap in mercy; break up your fallow ground: for it is time to seek the LORD, till he come and rain righteousness upon you." (Hosea 10: 12)

"It was but a little that I passed from them, but I found him whom my soul loveth: I held him, and would not let him go, until I had brought him into my mother's house, and into the chamber of her that conceived me." (Song of Solomon 3: 4)

Dear Lord God, my search is over! I've look high and low. But I could not find anyone who unconditionally, without malice and contempt, truly loved my soul like you do! I will never leave you, nor forsake you! I am yours, FOREVER!

Notes, Reflections, and Revelations

Chapter 6

A Passion for Relationship

The zeal and passion of God for a renewed relationship with man is exhaustively addressed throughout the Holy Bible. The Scriptures contain the expressed thoughts of God relative to the fulfillment of His plan to be joined with man eternally. The concern, love, and passion God has for humanity is painstakingly outlined in the Word of God. The veil of eternity is soon to be pulled away and the passion of God shall be fulfilled and completed.

It is vital for us to understand the extent and nature of God's passion for humanity. Jesus Christ and His completed work at Calvary provide a capricious illustration of the aforementioned passion of God. Of particular note, consider the letter written by Saint John, a close disciple of Jesus Christ. Relative to the reconciliation between God and man, John details (Chapter 3: 1-21) a critically important encounter between Jesus Christ and a Pharisee whose name was Nicodemus. As a Pharisee, Nicodemus was known to be a devoted, learned, and faithful Jew, a member of the

Sanhedrin court according to the report of John.

The Pharisees were a group of Jewish teachers and leaders who provided counsel and guidance as it pertained to the governance of the daily affairs for Jews of the day. It has been suggested by biblical scholars, particularly in relation to the state of Judaism during the period of Christ's earthly journey in human form, that Nicodemus represented a unique minority within the contingent of the Sanhedrin Court of that time. He appears to have been a man who, either through thorough research of the Jewish law and the writings of the Prophets, or via observed "empirical" evidence of miracles and divine manifestations; was willing to proscribe veracity and legitimacy to the teachings and preaching of this man (a carpenter's son) heretofore known as Jesus of Nazareth.

Biblical scholars varyingly debate the true motive(s) and purpose for which Nicodemus sought audience with Jesus. The report of John indicates Nicodemus came in the night, under the cloak of darkness, presumably to avoid detection by his colleagues and peers. The prospect of gleaning the materials fruits and benefits associated with an alliance with Jesus were far too enticing for Nicodemus to ignore or neglect. This is all too often the same motivation for many people today. Nicodemus, comparable to a vast contingent of people living in contemporary times, could be categorized as being unredeemed, unrevived, and generally spiritually destitute. He sought redress of his plight in Jesus Christ!

Thousands and perhaps even millions of people flock to churches around the world, in pursuit of the promise of deliverance from their lives of poverty and despair. Like many of the Jews living during the life and times of Jesus Christ, the demands of their carnal nature and fleshly appetites compel them to seek refuge in the presumed providence of the incarnated God. Thus, their primary motivation is satisfying the flesh's appetite for temporal pleasures.

Assuredly, God is concerned with our temporal plight and condition. The Scriptures emphatically validate this contention. Note the following:

"Beloved, I wish above all things that thou mayest prosper and be

in health,…" (3 John 1: 2 a-b)

This verse is liberally transliterated, and rightfully so if done judiciously and theologically- correct, by many as clear evidence that earthly health, wealth, and prosperity are God's ordained will for those who love and worship Him. Thank God for His liberal distribution of health, wealth, and material prosperity upon His people!

However, with respect to the portion of Scripture noted above, it is imperative that we use caution not to terminate our reading, and thus, our understanding of the divine will of God before completing the thought articulated by John. The latter clause of the verse reads:

"…even as thy soul prospereth." (3 John 1: 2 c)

One of the operative words in that clause is *"even"*. Parenthetically speaking, the word *"even"* in the clause can be translated to mean "likened unto" or "after the same manner". Essentially, pursuit of a "prosperous" soul should always take precedence over our temporal prosperity or accumulation of material gain. We must keep our priorities in order!

The efforts and deeds of God relative to His involvement with humanity far exceed the scope and realm of the temporal world. God's vision for humanity can't be confined to the limitations of our finite minds and ideas of fulfillment. God has crafted an eternal existence on the illustrious canvas of His eternal mind, exceeding the breadth of anything we can begin to imagine or contemplate.

Based on the information provided by Saint John, we can extrapolate or surmise a great deal about Nicodemus' primary motivation from the second verse of chapter three:

"...Rabbi, we know that thou art a teacher come from God: for no man can do these miracles that thou doest, except God be with him..."

Evidently, Nicodemus had some inclination that Jesus was not a normal man. The performance of unfathomable miracles and deeds on the part of Jesus undoubtedly persuaded and convinced Nicodemus and assuredly others that this was no ordinary man. Jesus Christ, the possessor of all knowledge and wisdom discerned and understood the true nature of Nicodemus' request for an audience with Him.

The reputation of Jesus preceded him throughout the land. From the very inception of Christ's earthly ministry, there was undoubtedly an oral record of His wondrous works. His healing of the infirmed, conferring of sight to those who were blind, cessation of a woman's lifelong menstruation of blood, and transformation of everyday water into wine by the mere spoken word of Jesus are but a few of His recorded miracles.

In contemporary times, people are likewise drawn to women and men whom God uses to demonstrate His divine authority over all of Creation. As instruments of God, healing and deliverance is exacted upon the lives of those possessing and exercising faith in the power and sovereignty of the Almighty. Men and women passionately desire to have the void and emptiness pervading their lives eradicated and replaced with some measure of hope and fulfillment.

People are starving for healing and deliverance. And like the woman with the issue of blood are willing to expend all of their "living" in desperate pursuit of a solution to their dilemma. Use of illicit drugs and other substances, unbridled sexual encounters, acquisition of money, houses, land, companies, and corporations ultimately prove to be insufficient when it comes to satisfying the lack of their weary hearts and souls!

The solution to one's predicament can't be "completely" obtained through the tangible, material possessions attainable in the World. Inarguably, the human franchise is capable of providing some temporary relief and satisfaction. However, it is critically important that we note the response of Jesus to the inquiry of Nicodemus on the occasion recorded by John. Jesus seems to infer the following in His response to Nicodemus: "I (*Jesus*) **know** thou were drawn to seek audience with me because of the unexplainable feats that have been attributed to me. But I have something far more valuable to offer you".

Presumably, the reputation of Jesus Christ was enhanced by the many people who likely attested to the fact their lives had been positively affected by the demonstration of God's power and authority (miracles, healings, and great works). In the presumed words of Jesus Christ, "Nicodemus you are to be applauded for your desire and earnest interest in the tangible manifestation of my divine authority.

But there is far more to be gained from this encounter than you can begin to imagine." Essentially, Jesus articulated to Nicodemus, and by proxy to everyone (both then and now) that will heed and act upon His admonition, the keys to a truly fulfilling and purposeful earthly existence. A "*relationship*" with God!

Men and women, boys and girls, as was the case with Nicodemus, are captivated by the mighty move of God through reports of His great miracles, works, and wonders! People marvel at the undeniable manner in which the Lord confers His favor upon the lives of those who have made a conscious decision to enter into a "*relationship*" with Him. Therefore, the earthly workmanship of Jesus Christ was deliberate and intentional. It's primary objective? To authenticate the veracity of the man, Jesus of Nazareth, the son of Mary and Joseph the carpenter, as the "*Christ*", "*the anointed One*"!

This relationship can be solidified by virtue of obedience to the mandates and instructions of Jesus Christ and His Apostles for the procurement of a *relationship* with God. It begins with faith, repentance, and identification with the Blood sacrifice of Jesus Christ. The response of Jesus to Nicodemus elucidates the primary message and focus of all of His earthly deeds and actions. *Relationship* with God! His response to Nicodemus intimates the focus and priority we all must embrace in our encounter with God through Jesus Christ!

Relationship with God is the one thing that will assure us of enduring and eternal fulfillment. Saint John implies that Nicodemus was enthralled with Jesus Christ because of the temporal impact Jesus demonstrated in the lives of people. In a large measure, untold numbers of people are likewise drawn to the Christian faith because of the implicit and often ill-informed declarations of many purported promulgators of the Gospel message.

Far too many self-appointed representatives of Jesus Christ tend to overly emphasize His capacity to bestow temporal benefits upon people's lives. Presumably, these persons are well intended. However, their proclivity to tacitly suggest that *"relationship"* with the Judeo-Christian God is principally concerned with a guaranteed path to physical wellness, fame, fortune, and material prosperity is misguided and theologically inaccurate.

Without equivocation, true believers should embrace a divergent ideology relative to their Christian faith. Paul, in his letter to the Church at Galatia, suggests that true Believers embrace other more highly valued benefits (fruits of the Spirit) accrued from a committed relationship with God:

"But the fruit of the Spirit is love, joy, peace, lonsuffering, gentleness, goodness, faith, Meekness, temperance:"
(Galatians 5: 22-23, a-b).

True believers are more concerned with actualizing what David intimates as being the "tabernacle experience". Specifically, David extols the merits of being in the abiding presence of God:

"One thing have I desired of the Lord, that will I seek after; that I

may __dwell__ in the house of the Lord all the days of my life, to behold the beauty of the Lord, and to __enquire__ in his temple."
(Psalms 27: 4).

An appreciation of David's attitude is best understood through a view of his context. David penned this psalm on the occasion of his flight from the wrath of his son Absalom. David articulates his longing desire to be back in the *Temple*, or *Tabernacle* of Jehovah, his covenant God. The Temple was a place where David could be assured the promise of the glorious presence of his God, his Protector, his Confidant, his Provider, and most importantly, the Keeper of his soul.

For David, much as is the case for us today, in response to the onset of great despair and life tribulation, came to a vitally important revelation. To *Tabernacle* with Jehovah is to cradle oneself in the warmth of God's loving concern. To *Tabernacle* with Jehovah is tantamount to commiserating with a close and valued friend. To *Tabernacle* with Jehovah is to be in ***relationship*** with God! This was the ardent motivation for the vast majority of David's actions, deeds, and exploits!

If we once again refer to the dialogue between Jesus and Nicodemus recorded by John, we can ascertain the process and formula for actualizing a true relationship with God, and vis a vis, the tabernacle experience. Note the completion of the dialogue between Jesus and Nicodemus:

" *Jesus answered and said unto him,* **Verily, verily, I say unto thee, Except a man be born again, he cannot see the kingdom of God.** *Nicodemus saith unto him, How can a man be born when he is old? can he enter the second time into his mother's womb, and be born? Jesus answered,* **Verily, verily, I say unto thee, Except a man be born of water and [of] the Spirit, he cannot enter into the kingdom of God. That which is born of the flesh is flesh; and that which is born of the Spirit is spirit. Marvel not that I said unto thee, Ye must be born again. The wind bloweth where it listeth, and thou hearest the sound thereof, but canst not tell whence it cometh, and whither it goeth: so is every one that is born of the Spirit.** (John 3: 3-8).

As a born-again, regenerated creation of God, we are granted the wondrous privilege of our souls serving as the

Temple or Tabernacle of *El Shaddai*. Paul affirms this when he admonishes all Christians in the following manner:

*"Know ye not that you are the **temple** of God, and that the Spirit of God dwelleth in you?"* (I Corinthian 3: 16)

The process of regeneration, solidified by the finished work of Jesus Christ at Calvary, ushered in a new phase in the creative work of God. The fracture and schism in the relationship between God and man was thereby redressed.

As regenerated creations (according to Paul, born-again Christians have become *"new creatures"*, see; 2 Corinthians 5: 17), our souls are transformed into repositories of the Spirit of God. When the Spirit of God enters our hearts and regenerates our souls, we become *"Temples"* of the Living God. In times past, God "moved" upon the hearts and minds of Man. However, the completion of Jesus Christ's earthly mission at Calvary completed the redemptive work that would foster reconciliation between Mankind and the Eternal God of Glory.

Now the Spirit of God resides in the hearts and souls of those who have identified with Jesus Christ through faith and placed their trust in Him as their Savior. The infilling of the Holy Spirit of God provides the recipient with "power" to actualize God's mandate for holiness and righteousness. Jesus Christ emphatically instructed His Disciples concerning the importance of this divine power. Luke quotes Jesus:

"And, behold, I send the promise of my Father upon you: but tarry ye in the city of Jerusalem, until ye be endued with power from on high." (Luke 24: 49)

The ongoing continuation and viability of our relationship with God is predicated upon our commitment to passionate pursuit of a lifestyle that is pleasing to God. We are not yet perfect. Nonetheless, the ardent pursuit of Godly "perfection" should be our primary motive as Christians. For this is pleasing to God!

Understanding the egregious and noncompliant nature of our flesh, God made provisions for our predicament. The dispensing of the Holy Spirit was/is designed to support our conscious effort to fulfill the appeal of God for us to live holy and righteous. Try as we might, our discipline, religion, and/or cognitive insights are generally ineffective as we attempt to live holy of our own volition and will. We need POWER! We need "The Spirit of God"! Heed the words of Jesus:

"But ye shall receive power, after that the Holy Ghost is come upon you: and ye shall be witnesses unto me both in Jerusalem, and in all Judaea, and in Samaria, and unto the uttermost part of the earth." (Act 1: 8)

The outpouring of the Holy Spirit in Jerusalem after the Ascension of Jesus Christ signaled the inauguration of the New Testament Church. The outpouring of the Holy Spirit "upon all flesh" was first evidenced by the "infilling" of one-hundred twenty souls, gathered together in the Upper Room on the day of Pentecost. It occurred precisely as was conveyed to the Disciples via the instructions of Jesus Christ preceding His Ascension.

The initial evidence that those souls had received the great promise of God (Joel 2: 28) was the manifestation of *"glossolalia"* or "many tongues". The report provided by Luke the Physician indicates those present;

"were filled with the Holy Ghost, and began to speak with other tongues, as the Spirit gave them utterance" (Acts 2: 4).

Metaphorically, this is likened unto the cry of a new born baby. It represents the initial sign that the Spirit has taken up residence in the recipient.

This was confirmation and fulfillment of an eternally orchestrated process of restoration on the part of God. The provision of the Holy Spirit was/is designed by God for women and men to avail themselves of the opportunity to *"tabernacle"* with their Creator. It introduced a new dispensation in God's involvement with humanity during the earthly experience of the latter.

The "new-birth" experience formula was initially articulated to Nicodemus (and others present) by Jesus Christ. The obedience to death by Jesus Christ when He was crucified on the hill known as *Golgotha* signaled the fulfillment of Christ's passion. The possibility of "rebirth" was thus assured. Accordingly, when one's "revitalized" soul is enraptured and activated by the power of the Holy Spirit, she/he is reconnected with God. Relationship is formed. Then, and only then, is the true *passion of man* fulfilled!

Daily Verses & Salutations

"And he sought God in the days of Zechariah, who had understanding in the visions of God: and as long as he sought the LORD, God made him to prosper." (2 Chronicles 26: 5)

"I sought the LORD, and he heard me, and delivered me from all my fears." (Psalms 34: 4)

"But Esaias is very bold, and saith, I was found of them that sought me not; I was made manifest unto them that asked not after me." (Romans 10: 20)

"As the hart panteth after the water brooks, so panteth my soul after thee, O God." (Psalms 42: 1)

My God and My Savior! Thank you for chasing after me with passion and zeal! Now that I've found you, I've no desire to leave your presence! You complete me! You are my joy, my passion, my water, my bread, my life!

Notes, Reflections, and Revelations

Chapter 7

Actions Speak Louder Than Words

Most Christians would emphatically agree that developing and maintaining a quality, committed relationship with God has been a wonderfully satisfying experience. Salvation, and thus a viable relationship with God, is the best decision we could ever make during our earthly journey. Temporal prosperity and success pales in comparison to eternally residing in the warm bosom of God's love.

Paul gives voice to the sentiment of most Christians:

"But what things were gain to me, those I counted loss for Christ. Yea doubtless, and I count all things but loss for the excellency of the knowledge of Christ Jesus my Lord:..."

(Philippians 3: 7-8a, b)

To know God, is to love God! To know God, is to adore God! To know God, is to obey God! To know God, is to know "excellency" and completeness!

There is an important facet of "knowing" or being in relationship with God that one would logically expect should be quite easy. What? Developing and sustaining constructive, productive, nurturing, supporting, encouraging, and resilient relationships with our fellow man.

Love and relationship with our "fellow man" can often seem elusive and painstakingly difficult. This can be true for the most ardent committed and mature Christian. Why is this so? A sundry list of factors seems to impinge upon our ability to actualize quality relationships with other human beings.

Volumes upon volumes, pages upon of pages of prose, literature, and other forms of instructional text have been dedicated to the building of quality relationships. Conflict and friction has been visited upon the earthly experiences of humans for ages. Beginning with the first recorded murder within the human family (exacted upon Abel by his brother Cain), the inability to resolve our differences and find a common ground of interest has plagued humanity.

The intent of God, via the workmanship of Jesus Christ, was to usher in a new season in humanity's earthly experience. The love demonstrated by God in the person of Jesus was partially intended to illustrate the process of achieving friendship, fellowship, love, peace and harmony with our "fellow man". If the love of God resides in your heart, love for your fellow man should be an expected and normal byproduct.

A wonderful aspect of God's character is His willingness to not simply declare His will and desire for our lives. For our God is not one to simply instruct and tell us how to perform a thing. He is willing to demonstrate and perform it personally. Thus, Jesus spoke the will of God; then He performed the will of God! What awesome love!

The Word of God declares that our love for God is demonstrated not simply via our spoken word. Assuredly, oral expression of one's adulation is urgently desired and important to God. Note the words of David:

> "To the chief Musician, A Psalm for the sons of Korah. O clap your hands, all ye people;

shout unto God with the voice of triumph." (Psalms 47: 1)

"My soul shall be satisfied as [with] marrow and fatness; and **my mouth** shall praise [thee] with joyful lips:...." (Psalms 63: 5)

"O give thanks unto the LORD; **call** upon his name: make known his deeds among the people." (Psalms 105: 1)

Many contend (rightfully so) that God is fully cognizant of their feelings towards Him. God knows and sees all things they'd argue. Outward, open, verbal expression of one's affinity for God is unnecessary they'd say. However, God, like any beguiled and smitten lover, swoons at the vocal expression of our adulation and fervent affection. He, like most people, longs for the admiring voices of those who love and adore Him.

The Word of God proffers a litany of illustrations to support my contention. As the various authors of the Holy Bible came to know God in an intimate way, they were moved to declare their affection for Him. Women and men of old, moved and inspired by the unction of the mighty power of God, penned their "knowledge" of a great God for whom they found to be worthy of their admiration.

The primary point I desire to articulate is basically reiteration of a previously inferred truth about our glorious God. In the form of His Holy Word, the Scriptures, God has provided us a template or model for sincere, committed relationship. Specifically, if you desire a clearer understanding of the process of developing and maintaining God-centered human relationship, simply consult the Word of God. God is the ultimate "role-model" of relationship!

God-centered human relationship consists of sincere "word" combined with sincere "action". Too often, Christians talk love, but fail to practice love! Have you ever been in relationship (at least that's how you referred to it!) with someone who constantly verbalizes their love and devotion to you? Admit it or not, everyone likes to be told that they're cared for. Loving words makes our heart happy and glad!

In that vein, David said it best via his expression of appreciation to God for the soul-stirring, heart-racing, and mind-comforting words imparted by God unto him.

Reflecting on David's metaphorical use of taste is exhilarating to the enlightened mind. Note his figurative use of the sense of taste in the following verse:

"How sweet are thy words unto my taste! [yea, sweeter] than honey to my mouth!" (Psalms 119: 103)

How many wives and husbands longingly ache to hear the sound of similar "sweet nothings" softly whispered in their ear from their companion? How many sons and daughters today long to hear wonderful words of approval and affirmation from their parents and/or guardians? Few would refute the power of soothing words upon the palate of one's mind, spirit, and heart!

Unfortunately, it is all too often the case that those professing melodious and endearing words of affection simply stop at the point of verbalizing their feelings. There is much talk, but sparingly little action supporting the veracity of their words. Such behavior speaks to a vitally important element of quality God-centered relationship. If you desire fervent and resilient God-centered relationship, companion your words with "deeds"!

Evidence of the presence of the true love of God is exemplified by word and deed! God always companions His Word, with deeds. As Christians, we are compelled to emulate the character of our God. The effectiveness of our witness to unbelievers, **and Believers**, is a direct function of our ability to be totally Christlike. In our thoughts, in our conversation, and in our actions we must exemplify Christlike virtue. Consider the following verses for embellishment of my assertion:

"And whatsoever ye do in word or deed, [do] all in the name of the Lord Jesus, giving thanks to God and the Father by him."
(Colossians 3: 17)

"My little children, let us not love in word, neither in tongue; but in deed and in truth." (1 John 3: 18)

Consider a fairly well known proverb. It is in direct accord with the principle of marriage between word and deed. *"Talk is cheap!"* Essentially, words are of marginal value if not supported by concurrent action. John elucidates this notion in the following manner:

"If a man say, I love God, and hateth his brother, he is a liar: for he that loveth not his brother whom he hath seen, how can he love God whom he hath not seen?" (1 John 4: 20)

John suggests in the latter verse that expressions of love for God are of little value if not coupled with corresponding action in the form of love for our fellow man!

We reside in a world rift with unfulfilled promises, unbridled lying, speaking of falsehoods, and what might otherwise fall under the category of "misappropriation of the truth" (simply another way to say lying). Such behavior is considered the norm today! In fact, in many circles, it is considered a readily acceptable and expected mode of behavior. Lying and manipulating facts is generally condoned and encouraged. Sadly, competent liars are often regarded as the paragon of success in many forums of today's world.

The depraved manner in which people mishandle

their word is only rivaled by their insipid attitude toward honoring their word with action, or the lack thereof. In other words, an outright lie or falsehood is bad enough. Couple this with a proclivity to promise action when a clear lack of intent to fulfill the promise never existed. Such conduct is abhorrent. This is in direct opposition to the will and character of Christ. This is not Christ like! God is displeased with the preponderance of this type of conduct.

God-centered relationship is founded upon an embracing of the full spectrum of behavior and conduct that exemplifies the character of Christ. This includes being a person of both word and deed. Can your friend, colleague, coworker, parent, child, sibling, neighbor, husband, wife, and most importantly, God; depend on you to comport yourself as a person of word and deed? How would they respond to this question?

Heed these solemn words from Paul in a letter to the Church at Corinth:

"Examine yourselves, whether ye be in the faith; prove your own selves. Know ye not your own selves, how that Jesus Christ is in

you, except ye be reprobates?" (2 Corinthians 13: 5)

Honoring our word with deeds is "proof" of our fellowship and allegiance to Jesus Christ as our Lord and Savior. It is "proof" and "evidence" that the Spirit of God lives and thrives in us.

Self-examination and introspection are crucial to our ability to fulfill our calling as earthly representatives of Jesus Christ. Know that people can only see the workmanship of Christ through us. Paul said:

"Ye are our epistle written in our hearts, known and read of all men:..." (2 Corinthians 3: 2).

As much as is within us, we must strive to be persons of word and deed. Strive to uphold a reputation that honors your God and Savior. To fulfill the latter requires conscious, diligent, and determined effort.

Failure is a distinct possibility! We all make mistakes! Mistakes are a function of our carnal nature. A sin or "fault" can befall the best of us. However, wholesale submission to the demands of your flesh and the influence of our enemy, Satan, is not an option. The ongoing practice of sinful behavior is antithetical to true Christian character. Such is the nature of those who are yet "sinners"! Therefore, give your word, and keep your word. Combine it with Spirit empowered action!

God has not prevailed upon Christians to perform something for which He has not equipped them. Such is not the nature of our God! As previously asserted, God always supports His "words" with corresponding action. If God requires something of us, He will likewise make provisions for our ability to perform it. Paul encouraged the saints in Ephesus accordingly:

"For it is God which worketh in you both to will and to do of [his] good pleasure." (Philippians 2: 13)

With respect to our pursuit of quality God-centered relationship, the serious nature of coupling our words and deeds can not be expressed too stridently. Continuity between our words and deeds is vital, particularly considering that our actions serve as a reflection of our affiliation with God. Your/my designation as "Christian" is tantamount to taking on the mantle of God's earthly representative. We bear the name of Christ!

The significance of bearing the name of Christ is that our words and deeds are constantly undergoing critical scrutiny. Much more is at stake than our personal name and reputation. Essentially, if people are unable to see the transformative power of God in our lives, via congruence between what we say and what we do, the cause of Jesus Christ (winning souls) is adversely impacted. John admonishes Christians as follows:

"But whoso keepeth his word, in him verily is the love of God perfected: hereby know we that we are in him. He that saith he abideth in him ought himself also so to walk, even as he walked."

(1 John 2: 5-6)

A thorough exegesis of this verse is in order. In the first clause John establishes the conditions or terms of a reliable litmus test of Christian fidelity to God. John establishes the argument that certain virtues and attributes are associated with true Christian allegiance. In essence, the perfected love of God is manifested in those who keep or honor their word. The word "perfected" as used in the clause verse is best understood to mean "completed". Perfected love is an attribute evinced in the lives of dedicated, spiritually mature Christians.

Note especially the words of John in the clause *"hereby know we that we are in him"*. Parenthetically stated, John says, "here is the proof (evidence) that we are in accord with and being directed by the Spirit of God". Those who profess affiliation with God and exemplify the love of Jesus Christ will *"...walk, even as he so walked"*. There is critically important relational fruit associated with conduct of this nature. TRUST!

The serious nature and affect of fulfilling this principle is captured in a very simple formula;

<u>*WORDS + DEEDS=TRUST*</u>

TRUST! The indomitable significance of this ingredient in any relationship is almost beyond the realm of descriptive words. Without trust, there is doubt, anxiety, apprehension, and most significantly, "fear"! Trust is the "cement" that bonds together a well-constructed and enduring relationship!

The next chapter addresses the vital influence of trust; both positively and negatively, on God-centered relationships.

Daily Verses & Salutations

"Blessed [be] the LORD, that hath given rest unto his people Israel, according to all that he promised: there hath not failed one word of all his good promise, which he promised by the hand of Moses his servant." (1 Kings 8: 56)

"Then said they, We will restore [them], and will require nothing of them; so will we do as thou sayest. Then I called the priests, and took an oath of them, that they should do according to this promise." (Nehemiah 5: 12)

"And, behold, I send the promise of my Father upon you: but tarry ye in the city of Jerusalem, until ye be endued with power from on high." (Luke 24: 49)

"And, being assembled together with [them], commanded them that they should not depart from Jerusalem, but wait for the promise of the Father, which, [saith he], ye have heard of me." (Acts 1: 4)

My Lord, My Friend, My Comforter! I appreciate you for the expression and performance of your many works on my behalf. When I was yet in darkness and ignorance, you still chose to keep your word! I will daily strive to emulate your kind affection and devotion to your promises! Selah!

Notes, Reflections, and Revelations

Chapter 8

The Formula for Relational Freedom

The construction of structures of any significance such as a three-story, 8,000 square foot home, a 100-floor office building, and/or a 20,000-seat arena require careful thought and consideration. Construction engineers for these types of projects spend many hours calculating and measuring the impact of a myriad of geological, mathematical, and physical factors. The potential repercussions; structural failure and loss of life, make poor planning and flawed design totally unacceptable.

Comparable care and consideration must be ascribed to the building of quality God-centered relationship. Like the above listed examples of structures, the quality of the final product is a direct function of several factors. Quality God-centered relationship demands conscientious planning, and perhaps most importantly, quality building materials.

Of the numerous building materials required for God-centered relationship, perhaps the most important one is "trust". A close companion to trust is "faith". I would submit to you that trust and faith are the perfect illustration of a circular, reciprocal relationship. Let me explain this in greater depth.

First, let's consider a definition of trust. According to Webster's Dictionary, trust is; *"assured reliance on the character, ability, strength, or truth of someone or something; one in which confidence is placed"*. The definition of faith is given as; *complete trust; something that is believed with strong conviction"*.

In God-centered relationship, as a person consistently delivers on their promises, accordingly trust in that person grows. Likewise will there be a reciprocal increase in your faith in that person. As faith increases, trust increases. Consider a snowball rolling down a mountain of moist, freshly fallen snow. There is an ever increasing growth in its diameter and girth. So is the conjoined marriage of trust and faith in a richly soiled, fertile relationship. One thrives on the others growth, and each increases in breadth and size as they feed on one another!

Again, as inferred in an earlier chapter, God has aptly articulated (via the Scriptures) and demonstrated (via the

Supreme Sacrifice of His Son Jesus) to every Believer and practitioner of Christianity His allegiance to the principle of trust. What God said He would do, He has performed the same. God always delivers the goods!

The number of illustrations outlined in the Scriptures to support my contention are too numerous to thoroughly addressed here. God's promise (covenant) with Noah, Moses, David, to the Jews and to the Gentiles corporately are but a few examples. For the sake of illustration, I will use the example of Abraham to elucidate this concept.

Paul in his letter to the Hebrews said the following about God's dealings with Abraham:

"For when God made promise to Abraham, because he could swear by no greater, he sware by himself, Saying, Surely blessing I will bless thee, and multiplying I will multiply thee. And so, after he had patiently endured, he obtained the promise."

(Hebrews 6: 13-15)

Abraham, at the ripe age of 100, by virtue of the birth of his son Isaac with Sarah, could personally attest to the trustworthiness of God to keep a promise. You can trust God! God always delivers the goods!

God's word has been tried and found to be true. God has provided food and sustenance for his people by raining "manna" (heavenly bread) from the heavens (Exodus 16). When thirsty, and there appeared to be no water available for their journey, God made provisions by producing water from a rock (Exodus 17). Against seemingly insurmountable odds, God gave the city of Jericho to Joshua and the Israelites (Joshua 6).

The cadre of illustrations and examples of God's great history of satisfying His promises serve to fortify our trust and faith in Him. His attentiveness to our continued faith in Him is indefatigable. Thus, we have incontrovertible evidence, which merits our confidence in His dependability and faithfulness.

Nowhere is the gravity of trust so incredulously embodied than in our hope and belief in salvation and eternal life. Nothing epitomizes trust in relationship like our hope and belief in God relative to those two promises. Through our identification with Jesus Christ as our personal

Savior, and thus our reconciled relationship with God, we are putting the utmost amount of trust in God.

Our experience with God, both past and present, gives us great consolation and confidence. God gave us a new nature, one of righteousness in place of unrighteousness! God gave us a new mind, one of godliness in place of ungodliness! God gave us a new attitude, a positive one in place of a negative one! God gave us hope, in the face of hopelessness and despair. God gave us peace in the midst of storms, winds, and raging seas! God always delivers the goods!

In contrast to our relationship with God, let us examine the manner in which trust, or the absence thereof, pervades and impacts our human relationships. Time and again, if you were to take a poll of people who've participated in failed relationships, invariably they will report a deficiency in trust existed(s). An absence or deficit in trust leads to a corresponding quotient of deficit faith in one's companion, partner, friend, and etc. Small trust, equals small faith, equals relationship retardation!

A critical impediment to our ability to trust, and

therefore actualize God-centered human relationships is the residual debris from aborted, fractured, and/or ill-conceived relationships from our past and present life experience. Oftentimes the "cancer" from these kinds of relationships has either gone untreated or is simply in remission. The cancer resulting from such relationships flourishes if left untreated. Consequentially, our entire system; body, spirit, and soul, become blighted and debilitated.

Too often, the salient issues associated with ill-conceived relationships are left unresolved. Invariably, we stridently attempt (often unsuccessfully) to salve the putrid secretion from the relational cancer with "homemade" remedies. Homemade remedies include pity parties, gossip parties, gatherings focusing on bad mouthing those who've wounded us, and self-medication (alcohol, legal and illegal drugs, etc.) just to name a few. Unfortunately, denial, suppression, displaced anger, resentment, bitterness prove to be the byproducts of our homemade remedies.

Sometimes we seek solace and consolation from well meaning friends and family. But too often, these "biased" advisers are like Job's friends (Eliphaz the Temanite, Bildad the Shuhite, and Zophar the Naamathite) unlearned, untrained, and out of touch with the mind and will of God. Counsel from friends and family typically only provide us with marginal, short-term relief or remediation from our woefully painful predicament.

The consequence of untreated cancerous relationships is the onset of a predisposition that subjugates the possibility of future healthy fruitbearing relationships. Distrust! Distrust is one of the most prominent and pronounced saboteurs of healthy, God-centered relationship. It is a voracious and spurious relational traducer.

In consideration of our relationship with God, distrust and vis a vis, a lack of faith is not founded upon sound reasoning or logic. There is absolutely no rational or spiritually-based rationale for distrusting God. God has only sought the best for us. His interest in us is only for our betterment.

In reality our lack of faith in God is based on a struggle first evidenced by Adam in the Garden of Eden. Adam's decision to partake of the forbidden fruit led to great detriment for him, Eve, and all humanity. Adam's decision was influenced by a problem that plagues many unbelievers and Christians alike. His unwillingness to relinquish "control"! Permit me the liberty to expound upon this issue.

Adam was created from the dust of the earth. Inarguably, the Scriptures indicate that he was formed and fashioned after the image and likeness of God. In other words, Adam's earthly body was fashioned after the model or pattern of God's personhood, Jesus Christ. However, Adam's body (like ours) consisted of earthly, soul corrupting materials. The corrupted composition of the materials used to construct our earthly houses has dire consequences for us all!

The pattern from which Adam's (and our) earthly house was formed is analogous to wax figures of people housed in a celebrity wax museum. The wax figure is a very close replica of the real thing. However, a replica or representation of the real thing is all that it will ever be. Those of us who've made our *"calling and election sure"* wait with baited breath for the day wherein our souls shall be *"clothed"* with "the real thing"!

One of the major problems associated with our

earthly houses is it's predisposition to disdain any form of restraint, constraint, submission, and/or control. The flesh, our "members", is in constant engagement with God over ultimate control of our will, drive, and nature. The Holy Spirit residing in us arduously strives to subjugate and countermand the fleshly demand for control.

The Apostle Paul lucidly illuminates the insidious, recriminate nature of our earthly houses (the flesh) in his letter to the Church at Rome:

"Now then it is no more I that do it, but sin that dwelleth in me. For I know that in me (that is, in my flesh,) dwelleth no good thing: for to will is present with me; but [how] to perform that which is good I find not." (Romans 7: 17-18)

Paul, like we so often do today, expresses the interminableness of his conflicted condition. The will or desire to do what is right is present. But the wherewithal to perform it seems to elude us like a fallen leaf whisked away in a strong and whistling wind. Paul continues in this vein with these verses:

"For I delight in the law of God after the inward man: But I see another law in my members, warring against the law of my mind, and bringing me into captivity to the law of sin which is in my members." (Romans 7: 22-23)

Seldom is this more evident for many Christians than in their struggle with issues of distrust, lack of faith, and the squeamish, unnerving notion of relinquishing "control". The confluence of all these issues and the vociferous effects of untreated cancerous relationships conspire to thoroughly incapacitate our unceasing yearning to be bonded and connected. Unresolved, they often have a deleterious effect on our current relationships with friends, family, spouses, and/or potential marital companions.

So how do you resolve this dilemma? Only the soothing balm of prayer, supplication, fasting, and thorough saturation of the healing presence of God through His Word can truly mollify the cancer from blighted relationships. You must seek out an audience with the one who truly loves you. You must allow God to perform radical surgery on your heart and mind! Only God can remove the cancerous tumors that debilitate and retard your ability to engage in loving relationships!

God is never pretentious nor distaining in His assessment of our dilemma. A sincere, contrite, and repentant heart and disposition are the conditions that activate the loving balm of God on our behalf. It is God who truly knows and understands the tumultuous and foreboding relationship journey(s) that you have and/or are currently trodden. Communion with God until recovery is complete must precede any attempts to initiate new or reestablish old human relationships.

Through prayer and supplication, your process of communication with God will be optimized. In many ways, developing a fervent prayer life is comparable to developing an exercise regiment. In essence, you must develop what I call a "prayer ethic". Start with small prayer sessions, say 3-5 minutes twice daily. Incrementally increase your prayer regiment each day. Incorporate "mini-prayer sessions" into your daily routine, during lunch, coffee break, etc. Set an ultimate goal (half an hour, one hour, two hours, etc.) that suits your spiritual growth needs. God will *"order your steps"* and give you direction relative to what will benefit you most.

You will become increasingly more in tune with the move and instruction of the Holy Spirit. You will notice a closer, more intimate walk with God. Your carnal man will become increasingly more subject to the influence and power of the Holy Spirit. Quite obviously this is the conclusion Paul ultimately surmise in resolution of his contemplation of the power of the carnal nature residing in us all. He summarizes as follows:

"O wretched man that I am! who shall deliver me from the body of this death? I thank God through Jesus Christ our Lord"
(Romans 7: 24, 25a)

There is another important step in the process of activating and/or rehabilitating your capacity to trust and ultimately surrendering control of your heart in pursuit of human relationship. Basically it entails an expansion of the concept of surrendering control. It is the concept of "forgiveness".

The supreme example of forgiveness, like trust and faith, is found in an examination of the nature of God. Against every logical and rationale precept whereby one might forgive another, God defied all logic. Logically, the mere fact that God chose to forgive us makes absolutely no sense. In fact, all of the evidence and supporting documentation in our relational trial with God seemed to clearly mandate that He'd turn His back on us forever.

God had every right not to forgive us! But in forgiving us God desired to serve as a role model for us. The fact that God chose rather to forgive us elucidates a vital aspect of forgiving that escapes most people. Forgiving is about surrendering! Forgiving is about power! Forgiving is about control! Forgiving is about acquiring control by releasing control!

How does one acquire control by releasing control? When one chooses to forgive, essentially you are exercising the power to release and relieve yourself of poisonous, cancerous, and negative energy. The hurt and pain inflicted upon you by that person was/is a catalyst for hatred, bitterness, and resentment. All of those vile byproducts are tantamount to a type of sulfuric acid, eroding your heart, mind, spirit, and eventually, your soul!

Like God, by all rights, you can always find good reason and justification for choosing not to forgive. Sadly, your decision to retain the right to not forgive only serves to give power and control to the enemy of your soul, the flesh. God demonstrated the power of love and forgiveness by surrendering to Man control of his own destiny. True healing and deliverance comes when you retain control by surrendering control! That is exactly what God did! Surrendering has its benefits!

Take note of this liberating epiphany and admonishment articulated by Paul to the Church at Colosse:

"Forbearing one another, and forgiving one another, if any man have a quarrel against any: even as Christ forgave you, so also [do] ye." (Colossians 3: 13)

The ability to forgive is therapeutic. I have personally experienced and witnessed this notion. It can function as the healing balm of a broken heart. Forgiving is like the valve on a high pressured piece of plumbing. When you learn to forgive, you are opening the valve to heart and releasing the pent up, toxic debris of pain, hurt, and agony!

Forgiving is therapeutic to the troubled and distraught mind. The wounds left from fractured relationships, if not properly treated, remain open and subject to infection. Fear and doubt are forms of infection produced by open, festering wounds of the mind. The mind then becomes vulnerable and a fertile breeding ground for open attacks by the enemy of your soul, Satan!

Forgiving is a form of cleansing for the heart that has been ripped and torn asunder. Like an antibiotic for infection or radiation therapy for a cancerous, malignant hematoma, forgiving is a reliable form of healing therapy for the mind. Ample and repeated doses may be necessary! Don't hesitate to use forgiveness often and liberally!

Above all else, forgiving is a theologically based tenet of our faith as Christians. Specifically, forgiving is a commandment from God. Consider the following verse:

> *"Judge not, and ye shall not be judged: condemn not, and ye shall not be condemned: forgive, and ye shall be forgiven:…."*
> (Luke 6: 37)

Forgiving is an act of faith! Forgiving is an act of unselfishness! Forgiving is an act of love! Love for your fellow man and by proxy, love for God!

Counseling and ministering to those who've previously or are presently consumed with the heart wrenching ravages of relational dysfunction is challenging work. In a large majority of cases, great harm and damage has been exacted upon either one or both parties prior to their seeking out help. I have personally witnessed individuals imprisoned by the shackles of great bitterness, resentment, and sorrow!

Admonishing and encouraging individuals to embrace and practice forgiving is one of the primary therapeutic interventions I have used as a psychotherapist. In general, I submit to them (and you) that forgiving is the basic starting point from which truly effective relational therapy emanates. When pride and ego are subjugated, one can move towards forgiving. Forgiveness is then applied to the wounds of a broken heart and troubled mind. Healing can then commence!

As is often the case, one's effectiveness in fostering a willingness of others to engage in a thing, it helps if you've personally practiced what you are preaching. There is a saying, "what's good for the goose, is good for the gander". Remember, God never demands anything of us that He Himself was not willing to likewise do. Note the following from the Apostle Paul:

"For we have not an high priest which cannot be touched with the feeling of our infirmities; but was in all points tempted like as [we are, yet] without sin." (Hebrews 4: 15)

We are without excuse! As the verse above intimates, nothing we might experience, as egregious, wicked, and horrific as it may appear to be, can compare to what our Lord and Savior has endured. Jesus Christ had the sins of all humanity heaped upon his "human" shoulders. He bore the pain, humiliation, and searing agony of sin. Yet He still chose to love and forgive us. What awesome love!

We must make every effort to practice what we preach to others. In those instances (we all face them at some point of our earthly journey) when the volition to exercise forgiving seems incomprehensible or elusive I offer you these sincere words of encouragement. Remember the price Jesus Christ paid for your salvation and deliverance. Inarguably, that price far exceeds the worth of your insignificant ego and pride. Let go, let God, and let the healing begin! Amen!

Daily Verses & Salutations

"Preserve me, O God: for in thee do I put my trust."

(Psalms 16: 1)

"The LORD is my rock, and my fortress, and my deliverer; my God, my strength, in whom I will trust; my buckler, and the horn of my salvation, [and] my high tower." (Psalms 18: 2)

"How excellent [is] thy lovingkindness, O God! therefore the children of men put their trust under the shadow of thy wings."

(Psalms 36: 7)

"Trust in the LORD, and do good; so shalt thou dwell in the land, and verily thou shalt be fed." (Psalms 37: 3)

"Commit thy way unto the LORD; trust also in him; and he shall bring [it] to pass." (Psalms 37: 5)

"And he hath put a new song in my mouth, [even] praise unto our God: many shall see [it], and fear, and shall trust in the LORD."

(Psalms 40: 3)

Dear Lord, teach me how to trust! Help me with my struggle with faith and confidence! Neutralize my stagnating, debilitating, and festering propensity to distrust! Help me to let go! Assure me and console me, as I learn to release my volition and control unto YOU!

Notes, Reflections, and Revelations

Chapter 9

Nurturing the God-Centered Relationship

God-centered relationship, with God or Man, is founded upon definitive and specific terms of agreement. Essentially, the respective parties of God-centered relationship enter into a covenant arrangement. Adherence to the terms of the arrangement fosters the ongoing success of the relationship. Violation and abuse of the terms of the arrangement could ultimately lead to its demise. Consistency, stability, and harmony over the span of the relationship greatly contribute to its success!

The parallels between quality God-centered relationship, whether with God, or your fellow man are inextricable. One's ability to sustain successful God-centered relationship is a function of critically important issues. Attentiveness to ongoing maintenance and enhancement of the relationship is a prime determining factor best described as "relational efficacy". A more in-depth discussion of this concept is in order.

Our ability to fully appreciate the concept of

relational efficacy is best understood via thorough consideration of the terms upon which God-centered relationship was founded. God's perception of relationship is diametrically opposite to that of the secular world. Particularly, the level of devotion and commitment expected by God differs from most human relationships. Perhaps the best illustration of true God-centered relationship is the "engagement period" which commonly precedes the joining of a woman and man in marriage.

Consider this. In general, prior to a man and woman formally entering into the state of "holy-matrimony", an agreed upon space of time which precedes the date wherein the couple exchanges vows and consummates their union. This engagement period is a vitally important season for the two individuals, both short-term and long-term.

This space of time is generally dedicated to planning the details of the formal marital ceremony, the wedding. Invariably, depending upon the family structure, culture, and/or the background of the two individuals, announcement of the engagement is occasion for great celebration and revelry. As such, the engagement period often portends the excitement and great anticipation of the eventual union of the committed parties.

Nonetheless, the engagement period has far reaching implications for the two committed parties. The engagement period serves as a type of "trial" of the enduring commitment between both parties. It should be entered into "advisedly". Engagement is sacred! It is equally as sacred as the ultimate marital union.

The committed parties must understand and embrace the sacredness of this period. There is much at stake. Negligence of the seriousness of the agreement could have grave and dire repercussions for either one, or both parties. Essentially, they have entered into a "hallowed" agreement. Another term ascribed to the engagement period is "betrothal". Betrothal is a very serious matter in the economy of God.

What is the relevance of betrothal in the economy of God? First of all, a definition is in order. Betrothal is "a promise to marry". Betrothal is a sacred agreement or covenant. It is established and founded upon the integrity of the "solemn word" of two parties to honor the agreement.

Betrothal serves as an expression of fastidious observance and adherence to the terms of the commitment. It infers a conscious and informed decision to vanquish all interest in other persons vying for your attention. Your focus is only for the affections of "the" one with whom you are now betrothed!

Betrothal is a concept all too often misunderstood and/or completely neglected in many sectors of our contemporary, secular, and unfortunately some Christian-based forums. For many, it is simply a tradition or optional formality. It is perceived to be an outdated and insignificant aspect of many religious dogma and/or teachings. People treat betrothal very casually. Quite frankly, the biblical basis for betrothal is sacred, enduring, and eternal.

In reality, betrothal is a "type" or metaphor for a special bond and agreement we have with God by virtue of our identification with Jesus Christ as our personal Savior. It represents a sacred and holy "spiritual season" of our eternal existence. Betrothal between the Christian and God begins a microsecond after the rebirth process is complete. Betrothal culminates with all those who've been redeemed and reconciled with God coming together as one collective; the Bride.

The significance and urgency for "faithful" attentiveness to betrothal with God is noted in the following verses:

"And I John saw the holy city, new Jerusalem, coming down from God out of heaven, prepared as a bride adorned for her husband. And I heard a great voice out of heaven saying, Behold, the tabernacle of God is with men, and he will dwell with them, and they shall be his people, and God himself shall be with them, and be their God". (Revelation 21: 2-3)

Clearly, betrothal is a very serious issue with God. You would never know it to examine the predominant experiences of many secular (as well as many purportedly Christian) couples during betrothal. Contemplate the typical secular conception of betrothal. In most cases, what was intended as sacred spiritual season is simply a time for ruminating about the frivolous details pertaining to the wedding ceremony.

In the vast majority of cases, the focus of betrothal tends to be on the following issues:

1. Who shall I choose to be my maid of honor/best man,
2. Which of my friends should I select to be members of the bridal party,
3. Finding the perfect location for the wedding ceremony,
4. Deciding upon who shall preside over the wedding ceremony,
5. Selecting the coordinator of the wedding,
6. Choosing a color scheme,
7. The style of dresses and tuxedoes for the bridal party,
8. The type of dresses and tuxedoes for the parents of the Bride and Groom,
9. Where the mother of the Bride is going to sit,
10. Where the mother of the Groom is going to sit,
11. Who to select to sing the songs during the wedding ceremony,
12. Etc., etc., etc., etc.

Who would dare argue or challenge the relevance and importance of these details? Certainly not I! In fact, attention to details should always merit serious consideration. God, in particular, is imminently concerned with detail.

Indisputably, order, organization, and preparation are vital elements of the character and eternal economy of God. God is also an interminably, hopeless romantic! This is evidenced throughout the Scriptures. I have particularly noted this in my prior elucidation of the Song of Solomon. Thus the romantic side of God is greatly concerned with such details as the color, fabric type, length, and embroidery of the train flowing from His beautifully attired Bride!

One's attention to seemingly incidental wedding details such as attire, floral arrangements, decorations, color scheme, and other ancillary accoutrements are certainly in order. The Scriptures highlight the great attention to detail demonstrated by God with respect to His range of interactions with humanity. Likewise, physical beauty and splendor are important to God. God is an irreverent purveyor of all beauty and splendor. God was/is the Master Architect of all beauty and splendor! The heavens and earth resolutely proclaim the beauty, wonder, and splendor of God's great and illustrious works.

The Scriptures contain countless illustrations of this

point. Note God's instructions to Moses:

> "And thou shalt make holy garments for Aaron thy brother for glory and for beauty." (Exodus 28: 2)

And the instructions from God, first given to David, and later fulfilled by Solomon:

> "And he garnished the house with precious stones for beauty: and the gold [was] gold of Parvaim. He overlaid also the house, the beams, the posts, and the walls thereof, and the doors thereof, with gold; and graved cherubims on the walls." (2 Chronicles 3: 6-7)

And the vision of the holy city of heavenly Jerusalem described by John the Revelator:

> "And he carried me away in the spirit to a great and high mountain, and shewed me that great city, the holy Jerusalem, descending out of heaven from God, Having the glory of God: and her light [was] like unto a stone most precious, even like a jasper stone, clear as crystal;…" (Revelation 21: 10-11)

God's meticulous attention to the slightest of details is irrefutable. Nowhere is God's appreciation and interest in beauty more lucidly demonstrated than in a portion of the verse noted earlier in this chapter (Revelation 21: 2-3);

"prepared as a bride adorned for her husband".

Here, God is likened unto any Bridegroom who longingly gazes upon the beauty of his Bride with pride and admiration. Clearly, this clause, and so many other Scriptures bear witness of God's appreciation and concern for aesthetics.

Nonetheless, we must not lose sight of an important fact. It is not simply the exterior beauty of the Bride for which the Bridegroom is enamored. The "inner man" is God's primary concern. This is aptly elucidated via the record of Samuel as he sought to identify God's "chosen King", Saul's replacement as King of the Israelites. Note the following:

"But the LORD said unto Samuel, Look not on his countenance,

or on the height of his stature; because I have refused him: for [the LORD seeth] not as man seeth; for man looketh on the outward appearance, but the LORD looketh on the heart." (1 Samuel 16: 7)

This verse illuminates a salient point with respect to relationship. Far too often our lives (both Believers and unbelievers) are consumed with an emphasis on form, fashion, and appearance! Appearance is often our number one priority! We exact an inordinate amount of time and energy on fostering a well orchestrated "show" or "performance" in an attempt to garner the approval of onlookers. Such is the case for far too many people during the betrothal period.

Unfortunately, as is inferred in the verse above, with man a "heart" which seeketh after the things of God is not a primary focus. This is particularly true during the betrothal period. Often, either one or both parties have the attitude that the process of "wooing" and "charming" their betrothed one is complete. The objective, betrothal, a promise to marry, is complete. Presumably, there is no further need to expend the time and energy to "impress" their betrothed one. With

God, this is not so! Betrothal is only the beginning!

The gravity of betrothal is much deeper than most people understand it to be. Betrothal, to a great extent, has far reaching implications for the ultimate goal of marriage. Betrothal is a test of fidelity! Betrothal is a test of dependability! Betrothal is a test of sincerity! Betrothal is a test of one's fortitude and resiliency! Betrothal is a test of LOVE!

All too often, "love" is a term bantered about and expressed with languid passion and unabashed temerity. The basest forms of companionship (e.g. casual sex, premarital sex, partner swapping, partner sharing) are egregiously misappropriated as acts of "love". But with God, this is not so!

The kind of love by which God-centered betrothal is founded upon is vastly different. It is a kind of love that transcends the temporal nature of pleasure and passion. It supersedes the putrid physical gratuitousness people chose to engage in. Untainted and undefiled betrothal love is an interminable precursor to true marital bliss. Betrothal love is a true gift from God!

Moreover, betrothal gauges the limitations and boundaries of one's purported love and fidelity when sexual pleasure (another gift to man from God) is removed from the affinity equation. In essence, how will you deal with your companion outside of the bedroom? A test of this magnitude simulates the very nature of the vast majority of interaction time between a husband and wife. This is the true measure of one's love for your betrothed one!

Many have taking occasion to expound upon the virtues and attributes of love. Incalculable amounts of prose, song, film, theatrical productions, and other forms of creative works have been dedicated to the aim of overt expression of the concept of love. Many a besmirched suitor has earnestly attempted to convey the fervency and veracity of their amorous affections to another. Metaphorically, using the illustration of the woman with the issue of blood (Matthew 9: 20, Mark 5: 25, and Luke 8: 43), many have exhausted all of their "living" or tangible forms of currency in pursuit of the attention of one for whom they feverishly seek affection.

However, the Scriptures provide us with the most

cogent description of true love in action and in deed, as opposed to love in word only. For example, in various places, David ardently articulates his God-inspired conception of betrothal love. Consider:

"O love the LORD, all ye his saints: [for] the LORD preserveth the faithful, and plentifully rewardeth the proud doer."
(Psalms 31: 23)

"Let all those that seek thee rejoice and be glad in thee: let such as love thy salvation say continually, The LORD be magnified."
(Psalms 40: 16)

"I love the LORD, because he hath heard my voice [and] my supplications." (Psalms 116: 1)

"Consider how I love thy precepts: quicken me, O LORD, according to thy lovingkindness." (Psalms 119: 159)

Jesus Christ also attempted to articulate to His Disciples what viable, fervent, and active love looks like:

"Jesus said unto him, Thou shalt love the Lord thy God with all thy heart, and with all thy soul, and with all thy mind."
(Matthew 22: 37)

"Jesus answered and said unto him, If a man love me, he will keep my words: and my Father will love him, and we will come unto him, and make our abode with him." (John 14: 23)

The Apostle Paul adroitly elucidated what could be described as the "Manifesto of Love" for the New Testament Believer and practitioner of the true virtues of the Christian faith. Paul describes the attributes of "charity" which is also translated from the Greek language as "love":

"Charity suffereth long, [and] is kind; charity envieth not; charity vaunteth not itself, is not puffed up, Doth not behave itself unseemly, seeketh not her own, is not easily provoked, thinketh no evil; Rejoiceth not in iniquity, but rejoiceth in the truth; Beareth all things, believeth all things, hopeth all things, endureth all things. Charity never faileth:" (I Corinthians 13: 4-8 a)

And finally:

"And now abideth faith, hope, charity, these three; but the greatest of these [is] charity." (1 Corinthians 13: 13)

In summary, these verses capture the essence of true love. This kind of love is only derived from a devoted, resilient, and obstinate commitment to God-centered relationship. The consequence of commitment of this nature is an inviolably splendiferous betrothal with the Bridegroom, He who loveth your soul and gave Himself for you.

Fervent and sustainable relational efficacy demands that we continue to "woo" and "romance" the One who demonstrated(s) indomitable love for us. You should actively "romance" God daily! Send God a giant box of Godiva chocolates, a five-carat platinum ring, and a bouquet of long-stemmed, red roses with babies' breath to God today. How?

Bow to your knees, extend your hands to heaven, and cry out with a sincere and contrite heart, Lord, **"I Love You, today, tomorrow, and for eternity!"** Now live your life with a determination to zealously please your "betrothed one"! In doing so, you will likewise develop the acumen for romanticizing your earthly Bride/Groom, today, or in the future should God see fit to graciously bless you! Learn to love God, without compromise or condition. Then and only then will you be able to love your fellow man. For this is the will of God for you! Selah!

Daily Verses & Salutations

"But take diligent heed to do the commandment and the law, which Moses the servant of the LORD charged you, to love the LORD your God, and to walk in all his ways, and to keep his commandments, and to cleave unto him, and to serve him with all your heart and with all your soul." (Joshua 22: 5)

"I charge you, O daughters of Jerusalem, if ye find my beloved, that ye tell him, that I am sick of love." (Song of Solomon 5: 8)

"The LORD hath appeared of old unto me, saying, Yea, I have loved thee with an everlasting love: therefore with lovingkindness have I drawn thee." (Jeremiah 31: 3)

"Jesus said unto him, Thou shalt love the Lord thy God with all thy heart, and with all thy soul, and with all thy mind." (Matthew 22: 37)

"And now abideth faith, hope, charity, these three; but the greatest of these is charity." (1Corinthians 13: 13)

Lord, I love you! I love you for loving me! You are the lover of my soul! You are the true love of my life! Teach me, O Lord, how to **_LOVE_** you!

Notes, Reflections, and Revelations

Chapter 10

The Bond between Relationship and Fulfillment

"As the hart panteth after the water brooks, so panteth my soul after thee, O God. My soul thirsteth for God, for the living God: when shall I come and appear before God?" (Psalms 42:1-2)

In the verse above, and in numerous other places conveyed through writings attributed to him, David passionately intimates that nothing can provide his soul with true fulfillment and gratification in the manner **relationship** with God does. Therefore, it's easy to understand God's description of David as a,

"man after mine own heart" (Acts 13: 22).

David metaphorically describes his yearning for God via the clause *"panteth after the water brooks"*. Likewise today, whether consciously or unconsciously, the heart and soul of every woman, man, girl, and boy born into the world *"panteth after the water brooks"* of God.

Consider this. How does it feel when a negative incident occurs in your daily life that adversely impacts one of your valued human relationships? Dissonance between a wife and her husband, a parent and child, boyfriend and girlfriend, siblings, best friends, classmates, or coworkers can ruin one's day, week, month, or even year. Friction or conflict often precipitates heartache, anxiety, frustration and even depression. Fractured and damaged relationships are painful, hurtful and generally debilitating.

Thousands and perhaps millions of people seek out psychological or mental health services every day because of an array of problems or life issues. A common thread pervades the vast majority of cases whereby people choose to seek therapy or counseling. A direct correlation exists between the maladies they report and the preponderance of broken/fractured relationships in some aspect of their life experience.

The need to regain or restore harmony between oneself and a valued companion is often incessant. We are driven by an unabated need to find viable options for ameliorating the circumstances contributing to our relational disharmony. Only after we achieve relational balance and harmony are relief, happiness, and fulfillment restored to our innermost spirit.

Similarly, only when we find peace and harmony with God does our soul find sanctity, peace, and balance. A "relational compass" is wired to our souls! Prior to restoring harmony with God, our "relational compass" is in continuous flux and imbalance. The sinful nature every person is born with puts us at odds with God. The Apostle Paul suggests that prior to our spiritual regeneration; we were the "enemies" of God the Creator.

In the context of the entirety of humanity, our individual lives appear small and insignificant. We are likened unto drops of water, which at birth fall into the vast ocean of the earthly human experience. At the first point of entry, our drop creates a small, almost imperceptive ripple. The ripple our drop creates during our lifetime is but for a brief and fleeting moment.

After a short season, our drop ceases to be distinguishable from the innumerable drops of water which have coalesced, now constituting the ocean of humanity.

Quickly, inconspicuously, the ripple created from our drop dissipates and subsides. Its impact and influence quickly ceases and abates!

Ultimately our drop melds into an enormous collective, having realized its true passion. It is now a part of the collective of life, its purpose and meaning is achieved. We have found the passion of our soul. We've achieved perfect harmony, fellowship, and yes, relationship with our kindred, our brethren, our Creator.

The metaphorical use of the drop in the preceding paragraphs is an attempt to illustrate the relative impact of our individual lives in the context of the total tapestry of the human experience. Our journey on the Earth is basically short and fleeting. We know not how the length of time we shall reside on the Earth, nor how significant our lives shall be ultimately in the annals of human history.

Accordingly, note the following:

"Whereas we know not what [shall be] on the morrow. For what is your life? It [is] even a vapour, that appearerth for a little time, and then vanisheth away." (James 4: 14)

Therefore, it behooves us to make wise and prudent use of the time God grants to us in the earthly realm of our eternal journey.

Social astuteness and constructive interpersonal relations are important to most people. This assertion has repeatedly been validated through my experiences of counseling people from a wide range of sociocultural segments of life. In fact, most people who have been deemed as socially acrimonious and anti-social in the broad context of human interaction actually have a deep-seeded desire for positive and constructive relationships. They simply lack the capacity to actualize them!

Harmony with God is important to us. This is so because of the way God shaped and fashioned the original man. God made Man, Adam, in his image and *"after his likeness"*. We possess the capacity and desire for communion, just like our pattern, God. Our trichotomus construction, body, soul, and spirit afford us the ability to partake of the rich, full spectrum of God's wondrous creative works.

Our physical body allows most of us the privilege of experiencing a cacophony of exhilarating interactions via the use of our five senses, sight, taste, smell, touch, and hearing. Sight allows us to appreciate the beauty of a rainbow, colorful flowers, sunlight from the dawn of a new day, and the sunset of a day soon to be completed. Taste privileges us to appreciate and enjoy a meticulously prepared dish of Eggs Benedict, Chicken Marsala, a freshly broiled Maine lobster tail, a warm slice of apple, pecan, pumpkin, or sweet potato pie, a dish of delicately slice strawberries, melon, or pineapple.

The wondrous fragrance of a new born baby, of a meadow of wildflowers and daffodils, of a bouquet of roses, of a basket full of freshly washed linens is a privilege of great proportions that should never be taken for granted. The touch of smooth silk or cashmere on our skin, or the slight brush of someone's hand against our face by "the" one for whom we are deeply attracted can not be fully captured or described by the limitations of our words.

Finally, we have the sense of hearing. The essence of hearing can be gleaned from being in audience at a wonderful orchestral performance. The very angels of Heaven can appeared to be performing when a well-disciplined and Godly-anointed choir is assembled to minister during a worship service. The joys of hearing are embodied in the whispers of an admirer, words of adulation and admiration, ever so slightly and mildly perceptive, in the ear of her/him who is the object their affections. The glorious beauty of hearing is at its supreme best when our ears consume the cacophony of melodic sounds emanating from the symphony of birds, bees, crickets, and other like creatures inhabiting the Earth.

Unquestionably, our physical body is a wonderful gift from God. As elucidated above, our eyes, ears, hands, nose, and vocal cords facilitate the effectual operation of our five senses. But the totality of our existence transcends far beyond those five senses. In fact, the most critical component of our trichotomous structure that permits us to interact with our God and Creator. The soul!

Again, the physical body is a wondrously fashioned creation. But the splendor of our earthly body pales in comparison to the soul. Our earthly body was formed from the elements of the earth. Our soul was fashioned and formed from the enduring elements of the very essence of

God. The soul is eternal. The soul will have an eternal habitation. Either in the splendor of God's Glory, or the fiery, agonizing, tormenting place described by John the Revelator as the;

"lake of fire burning with brimstone" (Revelation 19: 20).

Regarding the earthly body, Paul said the following:

"Now this I say, brethren, that flesh and blood cannot inherit the kingdom of God; neither doth corruption inherit incorruption" (I Corinthians 15: 50).

This verse highlights a dilemma we face with respect to our earthly tabernacle. It should be valued, appreciated, and honored. It has the capacity to provide us with indescribable passion and pleasure. In the current dispensation of our existence, it affords the privilege of being able to interact with so many aspects of God's creative works.

As the verse above intimates, our earthly body has a crucial limitation. It has a short-term "shelf-life". In its current state, our earthly body is incapable of withstanding the rigors and demands of eternity. There is yet another limitation. Our earthly body possesses a limited capacity to interact with and be connected to God. However, God in all of His creative glory provided redress for this conundrum. God created the soul. Thus, was the possibility of eternal relationship with God achieved!

The soul residing in our earthly body has an insatiable affinity for companionship. The soul desires to be fawned over like a lovesick romantic. Our soul is infatuated and grossly enamored with the Spirit of God. The passion for God emanating from the soul is tantamount to the exhilaration one experiences via detection of the faintest whisper of soothing words emanating from the object of one's affection. The desire for God by our souls is likened to the feeling evoked when in the presence of a schoolboy/girl for whom we have a longingly wanton, secret crush.

God and the soul have a connection unlike anything else we can fathom in our earthly existence. Fulfillment for the soul is not possible in the absence of a bond with God. Try as we might, nothing else can compare to being reconnected with God. Millions will attest, to the indescribable and unfathomable experience of being in habitation with God via the indwelling of the Holy Spirit in our souls.

Without argument and controversy, many pleasures can be accrued via stimulation of the five senses of our earthly body. The arduous and determinate pursuit of physical pleasure by humans throughout the contemporary and historical world is testament to that assertion. However, true born-again, Spirit-filled, Spirit-led, faithful and committed Christians have been afforded an experience that is far sweeter and fulfilling. It's the glorious fruit of eternal relationship with God! Nothing else compares!

Daily Verses & Salutations

"The LORD hath done that which he had devised; he hath fulfilled his word that he had commanded in the days of old:"

(Lamentations 2: 17)

"And ye are complete in him, which is the head of all principality and power:" (Colossians 2: 10)

"He that hath the bride is the bridegroom: but the friend of the bridegroom, which standeth and heareth him, rejoiceth greatly because of the bridegroom's voice: this my joy therefore is fulfilled." (John 3: 29)

My God, My Friend, My soon coming King! I joy in the knowledge of your concern and care for me. Thank you for rescuing me! You have become my bridge over troubled water! There is none likened unto YOU! Now am I whole and complete! You have fulfilled the void of life! Selah!

Notes, Reflections, and Revelations

Chapter 11

<u>An Open Invitation</u>

"Behold, I stand at the door, and knock: if any man hear my voice, and open the door, I will come in to him, and will sup with him, and he with me." (Revelation 3: 20)

The conclusion of the whole matter is that God, in the person of Jesus Christ has garnered and satisfied His own just demands for spiritual vindication and justification. The blood Jesus Christ presented at the throne of God the Father was required to ameliorate the "relationship" schism between God and His beloved creation, Man. God, through Jesus Christ has done His part. Man must now make his choice!

While in exile on the island of Patmos, Jesus (*"one like unto the Son of man..."*, Revelation 1: 13) appeared unto Saint John the Divine to convey the true essence of His earthly deeds. An extensive dialogue between John and the Savior, delineated in chapters 1 through 3, is expounded upon. It is here that the Lord Jesus Christ provides a chronological record of the extreme measures God undertook in order to repair the breach in His relationship with Man.

The seven churches (Ephesus, Smyrna, Pergamos, Thyatira, Sardis, Philadelphia, and Laodicea) discussed in Revelation 2 and 3 represent the seven dispensations or "seasons" in the relational reconciliation journey between God and Man. This journey began with the "divorcement" between God and Man with the fall of Adam in the Garden of Eden. It culminates with the gathering together of every member of the Kingdom of God in the;

"new heaven and the new earth" (Revelation 21: 1).

The workmanship of Jesus Christ as a sacrificial lamb, culminating with His death, burial, resurrection, and ascension, ensured the provision of an opportunity for every person to achieve "relationship" with God. Relationship was thereby made available to all humanity. Faith and confidence in Jesus Christ, and identification with His shed blood, remits one's sin, making "relationship" with God possible once again.

At the end of Jesus' discourse with John in the third chapter of Revelation, He emphatically declares and appeals to all those who will hear and respond to His proclamation. In verse 20, the word *"behold"* indicates that Jesus is adamant and anxious for the reader/hearer to lend her/his attention to His declaration. In effect, He is saying, "listen, take note, and hear me out"! There is a sense of urgency conveyed by Jesus Christ to every person who desires to know the importance of His message!

In the very next clause of the verse He states *"I stand at the door..."* Jesus uses the first person pronoun "I" in the clause. The essence of this point is God left not the task of compelling men, women, boys and girls to respond to His appeal for reconciliation only to human representatives of God. God similarly chooses to shoulder the responsibility of "personally" soliciting mankind in the reconstruction of "relationship" with Him.

God greatly desires to know us on a personal and intimate level. So much so, that He left nothing to chance in the process of actualizing the reconciliation process. God, in the person of Jesus Christ, made all of the necessary provisions for garnering a renewed "relationship" with us. Every contingency and potential impediment to the actualization of that relationship has been accounted for. Oh what LOVE!

The second word in the clause "stand" is very insightful. To "stand" indicates that one is steadfast and determined in their purpose and mission. It suggests that one is resolute and not to be dissuaded. If one takes a "stand" for something, most assuredly there is no question about the merits and virtues of the cause for which one is pursuing. God undoubtedly believes in the cause of "relationship"!

Through Jesus, God's commitment to relationship with man has endured the test of time and innumerable generations. Since the fracture of His relationship with Adam, God has remained resolute and determined to be rejoined with us. God continues to "stand" in the face of our insolence, our stubbornness, our ungratefulness, our lack of appreciation, our disloyalty, most importantly, our unfaithfulness.

Through it all, God, the Almighty One, the Creator of all the known and unknown worlds, continues to *"stand"* to this day, waiting for us to respond to His overtures. How can we neglect so great an appeal for our attention? The Lord God "stands" in waiting, as a forlorn and unrequited lover. At this very moment, He longingly "stands" and awaits a response to His fastidious appeal from men, women, boys and girls around the globe.

The words in the same clause *"at the door"*, represents the location of the appealing suitor, God Himself. The word "door" is a metaphor for "heart". God stands knocking at the most treasured and valued part of our earthen vessels (houses), "the heart". His earnest plea to every woman, man, boy, and girl is quite simply, "won't you open up your heart that I might come in and commune with you?"

In closing, I would like to admonish you to enter into the sanctuary of hallowed "intimacy" with God. Without intimate relationship with God, emptiness, discontentment, and void will pervade your life. Through His Word, God has declared His providence and sovereignty over all Creation.

God is the Alpha and the Omega! The beginning and the ending! God fills all space and all space fills Him! Won't you let God fill the empty space and void pervading your heart? Only via God-centered relationship will you be able to honestly say, "I am complete"! God bless you always! Selah!

Daily Verses & Salutations

"I cried unto the LORD with my voice, and he heard me out of his holy hill. Selah." (Psalms 3: 4)

"In my distress I called upon the LORD, and cried unto my God: he heard my voice out of his temple, and my cry came before him, [even] into his ears." (Psalms 18: 6)

"This poor man cried, and the LORD heard [him], and saved him out of all his troubles." (Psalms 34: 6)

"In my distress I cried unto the LORD, and he heard me." (Psalms 120: 1)

"The name of the LORD is a strong tower: the righteous runneth into it, and is safe." (Proverbs 18: 10)

"Finally, brethren, farewell. Be perfect, be of good comfort, be of one mind, live in peace; and the God of love and peace shall be with you." (2 Corinthians 13: 11)

"Come unto me, all [ye] that labour and are heavy laden, and I will give you rest." (Matthew 11: 28)

Lord, I give you me! Selah!

Notes, Reflections, and Revelations

Printed in the United States
153981LV00003B/19/A